1/A

Dido

www.**davidficklingbooks**.co.uk

Also by Adèle Geras:

OTHER ECHOES

HAPPY EVER AFTER

TROY

ITHAKA

Dido

Adèle Geras

David Fickling Books

OXFORD · NEW YORK

31 Beaumont Street
Oxford OX1 2NP, UK

DIDO
A DAVID FICKLING BOOK 978 0 385 61517 4

Published in Great Britain by David Fickling Books,
a division of Random House Children's Books
A Random House Group Company

This edition published 2009

1 3 5 7 9 10 8 6 4 2

The Random House Group Limited supports the Forest Stewardship Council
(FSC), the leading international forest certification organization. All our titles
that are printed on Greenpeace-approved FSC-certified paper carry the FSC logo.
Our paper procurement policy can be found at www.rbooks.co.uk/environment.

Mixed Sources
Product group from well-managed
forests and other controlled sources
www.fsc.org Cert no. TT-COC-2139
© 1996 Forest Stewardship Council
FSC

Set in 12/15pt New Baskerville by Falcon Oast Graphic Art Ltd.

DAVID FICKLING BOOKS
31 Beaumont Street, Oxford, OX1 2NP

www.**kids**at**randomhouse**.co.uk
www.rbooks.co.uk

Addresses for companies within The Random House Group Limited can be
found at: www.randomhouse.co.uk/offices.htm

THE RANDOM HOUSE GROUP Limited Reg. No. 954009

A CIP catalogue record for this book is available from the British Library.

Printed in the UK by Clays Ltd, St Ives plc

This book is for Zahava Lever and Joanna Kramer

Elissa

You knew that you were in a dream when the edges of everything you gazed at were blurred and when figures bent and blended into the background and arrived and disappeared magically, moving in a way that wouldn't be possible in normal life. She'd been deeply asleep but now Elissa could feel herself floating up into wakefulness and the memory of her dream was leaving her. She blinked and turned over in her bed. There had been someone over there, by the door. Did he fly away? She tried to cling to what she'd seen: a slim man, wearing a strange-looking helmet. It had wings attached to it on either side, a little like an extra set of ears. Thinking this made Elissa start to giggle even though she was only half awake. Wings on his head and also on his feet. He'd hovered up and out of the door, and she most distinctly saw greenish feathers edged with gold, flapping gently at his heels as he rose up from the floor.

She'd even heard him speak but the words had disappeared almost entirely. 'Come, Maron,' she thought he'd said. 'Hermes cannot wait. You must come with me now.' Why was this winged creature speaking of Maron? She opened her eyes properly and leaned up on one elbow, forgetting her dream in the shock of seeing Tanith, her friend and one of the two girls with whom she shared this maidservants' bedroom, sitting on her bed, crying quietly – and yes, there was Maron with his arm around her. Men were not allowed anywhere near the women's rooms, and though Maron wasn't quite a man, he wasn't exactly a boy, and what did he think he was doing, whispering with Tanith while she and Nezral were sleeping? Well, I'm awake now, Elissa thought. Those two must have woken me up. Tanith's snifflings were growing louder and louder.

'Tanith!' Elissa whispered too, wondering how Nezral could sleep through the noise. 'Maron! What are you doing? Someone will come. What's the matter?' She got out of bed and went to stand in front of them. Maron, his gingery hair and sharp features making him look more than ever like a young fox, seemed sad. His smile, which could make the most churlish and bad-tempered person smile in return, was nowhere to be seen and his eyes were bright with unshed tears.

'It's happening,' he said. 'We're leaving. I have to go. Now. Tanith'll tell you. Goodbye, Elissa.'

He stood up, kissed the top of Tanith's head and ran out of the room.

'Tanith? Tell me what he said . . . please. When are they going?'

For a moment her friend did nothing but sniff and wipe her eyes. Elissa sat down on the bed beside her, overcome with sadness. Everyone in the palace knew this time had to come. From the day Aeneas had moored his ships in the harbour, the court gossips had been quite sure that he'd be on his way to somewhere else as soon as possible, but then he and the queen had fallen in love and for a while it seemed as though the Trojan and his crew would stay in Carthage for a long time. Then, more recently, everything became . . . Elissa couldn't name exactly what the change had been, but something was different, and lately the shadow of Aeneas' departure had hung over everything like a cloud billowing up and gathering darkness into itself before a storm. Dido's entire court – advisers, servants, hangers-on – had been wondering for days. They knew it would happen but no one could say exactly *when*, and now it seemed . . . But Elissa had to be sure. She said, 'Please tell me what Maron told you.'

'You heard him. They're leaving. They're down at the harbour. The ships are being loaded and prepared; they won't sail till tomorrow morning but Aeneas and his men are already at the dock. Maron says the queen took a sleeping draught so that she'd be spared the sight of him walking away from her, but how can he know such a thing? Oh, Elissa, what shall we do now they've gone? Maron . . . I'll never see him again.'

3

Tanith flung herself into Elissa's arms and sobbed. Elissa stroked her back and blinked back her own tears. Ascanius – even Aeneas' little son, who had been in her care since his father came to Carthage, hadn't been allowed to say farewell to her. Tanith moved away and found a cloth with which to wipe her eyes and nose. Her face was blotched with red from too much crying.

'Can we see them?' she said. 'From the window?'

Nezral gave a snore and a snuffle and turned over in her bed. Elissa and Tanith smiled through tears as they looked at their friend.

'She'd sleep through an earthquake,' Tanith said. 'Lucky Nezral.'

Their room was high up, on the first storey of the palace, above the kitchens. Leaning over the sill as far as she dared, Elissa could see a corner of the gardens, then a slice of the city: the yellow stone of the houses along the road that led from the palace to the harbour was almost glowing in the pale grey light just after dawn. The night, she thought, is hardly over and he's gone. He must have left in the dark, like a thief, creeping out of the palace. Not wanting to speak to anyone.

'There!' Tanith pointed. 'Behind the harbour master's house. Can you see?'

Elissa looked at the tiny, insect-like creatures moving in the distance. It was hard to believe that these were men, Aeneas' crew, loading his ships. Leaving. She gazed down on them for a while, unable to think or move.

4

Then a scream tore through the silence, ripping into Elissa's thoughts. It was horribly loud in the still air of the early morning and was followed at once by more screams, and then shouting and sobbing and a shrieking that sounded like a trapped animal.

'It's Dido. It's the queen,' Tanith said. 'Quick, Elissa, we must help her. Come.'

They ran down the steps to the main corridor of the palace and found Dido standing in the doorway of her bedchamber, her hair wild and tangled around her face, her eyes wide and horrified, her mouth agape. The Queen of Carthage, Elissa told herself, shrieking like someone demented. She was still screaming, but her words were clear.

'Master of the guard!' Dido's eyes blazed. She was beyond tears. 'Where in the name of all the Gods is everyone when I need them? Elissa! Tanith . . . Where are my courtiers? Where is everyone?'

Elissa and Tanith watched as, from all over the palace, they came running. The master of the guard reached Dido first.

'Madam,' he breathed, falling to his knees, 'I'm here. I'm at your service.'

'Then see to it that the bed in this room is got rid of. As soon as possible. I no longer want it here. Take it away. Now. As soon as you can gather enough men to carry it. Put it in the courtyard. You' – she turned to Elissa and Tanith and two other women of the household who had appeared in the corridor – 'all of you. Follow me, please.'

Dido set off down the corridor and Elissa found herself almost running to keep up with her. When the queen reached the chamber that used to be Aeneas', she flung open the door and stepped inside.

'Here,' Dido said, walking past the bed and into the adjoining room where he kept his armour and his clothes. 'Take these. Take everything.'

There were two trunks carved from sandalwood standing against one wall. The queen opened them both and a fragrance like old forests rose in the room. 'These are his shirts, his robes, his footwear, his sword – here . . . take them all and put them in the corridor outside. When the soldiers have dealt with the bed in my chamber, I'll give orders for them to come and help you carry out this rubbish.'

'But there's so much here, my lady,' said one of the serving women. 'And of excellent quality. There are many down in the city who'd be grateful for such garments.'

'No one will wear them. I'm going to burn them. I'm going to burn everything, every single thing that reminds me of him. All his possessions. They're tainted clothes. The leather and the wool and the fine dyes and the metal clasps and the rich embroideries – I want them destroyed, d'you understand?'

Dido sat down on a stool near one of the trunks and wiped tears from her eyes with a corner of her scarf. 'They're *my* things, if the truth be told. Mine. I gave him all of it. Every single thing in here: the garments, the weapons, the ships even. I'm the one who saw to it that the broken-down wrecks he sailed in on were made seaworthy again. I can't get the ships back. Maybe I'll make a sacrifice to Poseidon and beg him to send storms, to wreck my bastard husband on the rocks, which is what he deserves.'

She put her hands to her eyes and bent over, with her head nearly on her knees. Elissa could feel something in her own throat that was like a great lump of grief and sorrow. The queen began to moan. Elissa wanted to go and comfort her, just as she'd comforted Tanith, but her own sadness prevented her.

Another of the women came forward and said, 'Lady, don't cry. I'll take everything outside now. You'll feel better when you don't have to look at it any longer.'

Dido stood up. 'When you've finished in here, I want you to search through every single room in the palace. Collect everything – *everything* – that used to belong to Lord Aeneas, then take it to the courtyard, and when our accursed bed is in place, you can pile all his belongings on it.' She looked round at them and must have seen the horror on every face. 'And stop staring at me like that. I know exactly what I'm doing. I no longer wish to see a single reminder of Lord Aeneas anywhere near me. That's all. Go. I want this done at once.'

She swept out of her chamber, almost running. Elissa left the others to their work and ran after her.

Cubby

He knew that they'd only chosen him to carry the bed because he was strong and big for his age. If they'd wanted someone clever, they'd have taken any one of the other lads who did menial jobs around the palace. Cubby (he'd practically forgotten his real name) had a pretty good idea what everyone thought of him. They'd called him Cubby for two reasons. When he was small, he'd been fair-haired and lively and had bounced around the kitchen and the servants' quarters like a small animal. Like a lion cub, perhaps. That was what he liked to think. But it was also true that he spent his early days sleeping in a room that was as small as a cupboard and was used to store brooms and cleaning materials. So *Cubby* more probably came from *cupboard*. He'd stopped being like a lion cub when he got older and slowed down a little. He grew heavier and his hair became a kind of muddy brown and he had a round face and often looked puzzled.

They called him dim-witted: if not exactly backward, then certainly not advanced when it came to thinking clever things. As for speaking, he was useless at that and knew it and therefore generally kept his mouth shut and his thoughts to himself. He didn't have many friends – well, none really, until Maron fetched up at the palace with his master, Aeneas.

Maron had come into the kitchen on the very first day after the Trojans arrived and spoken to Cubby just as if he were a normal person who could chat and exchange jokes and banter like anyone else. Maron, Cubby thought, always said a pleasant word whenever he happened to bump into you. And now he wouldn't do that any more. Yesterday he'd come specially to see him. They'd sat down together on the bench near the kitchen door and Cubby couldn't stop thinking about what they'd said.

'We're friends, aren't we, Cubby?' Maron smiled at him. He had very white teeth and always seemed happy. He smiled a lot and his hair was gingery and stuck up all over his head.

Cubby nodded. Maron said: 'I'm going to tell you a secret, Cubs, but you mustn't say a word, right?'

'I won't,' Cubby said.

'That's why you're such a good person to tell things to. You don't blab, do you?'

Cubby shook his head. Maron went on, 'I've come to say goodbye. We're leaving tomorrow. And I didn't want to go without saying something. Didn't want you to find out about it later on.'

Cubby felt as though someone had come along and scooped out his insides. He'd seen the cooks pulling the innards out of lambs and chickens and wild boar but those animals were dead. He was alive so it really, really hurt, and when he'd got used to how much it hurt, he felt a hollow space where his guts used to be. He wanted to say: *Why do you have to go?* But somehow the words didn't come into his mouth in time, and Maron just carried on speaking. Cubby only half listened because it was hard to concentrate when you were feeling so bad.

'He says he has to go because the Gods have told him he must over and over again. Hermes has come to him many times, he says. Actually, I thought I saw Hermes once, just flying along down by the ships, but maybe I was dreaming. Anyway, we're off. And I have to go too. Ascanius . . . he's got attached to Elissa while we've been here, but before that I was like a kind of brother to him – know what I mean? And Aeneas will need some help with the kid, right? He's getting bigger every day and boisterous as a young puppy. You know that, Cubs.'

Cubby nodded. He would miss little Ascanius too. The child didn't seem to care that no one thought very much of Cubby and he used to come to the kitchen quite often, sometimes with Elissa, and if there were sweet cakes in the larder or just out of the oven, he'd steal one for the boy and move the others around on the tray so Cook wouldn't notice that anything was missing.

10

'So . . . I'm going to say goodbye now.' Maron stood up. 'We're off very early in the morning. Before you're awake.' He held out his hand and Cubby took it and they stood there for a bit, and then Maron flung his arms around Cubby and hugged him, and then he left the room and Cubby hadn't seen him again. He hadn't slept well and now he felt tired and sad because he knew Maron wasn't coming back. Not ever.

But then the master of the guard came to find him in the kitchen. He'd been right in the middle of bringing in some heavy sacks of flour from the storehouse, ready for the morning's baking, and when he'd finished doing that, there were the carcasses brought down from the market to dismember and hang up in the meat pantry. This was the coolest place to be because it was underground, but it smelled of congealed blood and you started to feel sick if you stayed there too long.

'You! The fat boy – I need you,' said the master of the guard.

'Me, sir?'

'You heard me. Drop what you're doing and follow me.'

'Yes, sir.'

'Best wash your hands first.'

Cubby dipped his fingers into a bowl of water that didn't look altogether clean but had to be a bit cleaner than his hands. The master of the guard said: 'That'll do. Come along. Haven't got all day.'

Things were mad after that. Not like daily life –

more like a dream where one thing happens after another with none of them making much sense. First he was led into the palace. He was almost pushed along the dim corridors, where flaming torches still burned in holders on the walls even though the sun had risen, and into a vast chamber, which was quite empty apart from a bed, standing in the middle of the floor. This was enormous. Four or five people could sleep in it, Cubby reckoned, and not bump into one another all night long. It was made from black wood, and the high bedhead was carved with patterns of flowers and leaves and other stuff he couldn't quite make out from where he was standing. Seven soldiers stood around the bed, which was spread with a fur coverlet and heaped with cushions at the end where someone's head might rest. He'd never seen such cushions in his life before. They were plump and soft and embroidered in threads of every colour, and just looking at them made Cubby want to lay his head on one of them and sleep for hours.

'Right. Let's move it. We're late already,' said the master of the guard. 'Orders are: out of here and into the central courtyard. Pick it up, men. You' – he pointed at Cubby – 'you go there, near the middle. Ready? One, two, three, *lift*!'

Cubby couldn't imagine why the queen would want a bed moved from a bedroom into a public courtyard, but he did know why he'd been picked. He was strong. They needed one more person to carry this thing. Fine, he was up for that. Made a change to be doing this instead of some boring task he'd done a thousand times before. Also, it took his mind off thinking about Maron. And he was with the soldiers so he could pretend to be one of them. For a moment a crazy dream filled his head. Maybe he'd do so well at this bed-moving lark that the master of the guard would say: *Leave the kitchen and come and be a soldier. I'll train you myself.*

So taken up was he with imagining his glorious career in the military that at first he didn't really notice where they were going. It was just one step after another, and as strong as he was, and even with seven other men bearing their part of the weight, this bed was a monster. His shoulder felt bruised already and they'd only just lifted the blasted thing off the ground and got it into the corridor.

Down one passage, then round the corner into another – it seemed to Cubby as though they were walking through a kind of maze. He'd never been any further into Queen Dido's palace than the kitchen and the corridors around it, and he'd never realized that it had so many rooms and turnings and spaces and halls. After taking what seemed like thousands of steps, they were in the courtyard. This was a giant version of what you'd have found in a normal house. It was so huge that it took quite a long time to walk across it from one side to the other. Cubby made up his mind to count his steps next time he wasn't carrying a bed. The courtyard was crowded with statues. Cypress trees and palm trees grew there in gigantic glazed earthenware pots, and right in the middle there was a raised circle paved with flat stones. In the middle of the circle, a fountain spilled its water into a wide stone basin. Cubby and the others manoeuvred the bed into position beside the fountain. Now that they'd got rid of the weight, the soldiers started whispering to one another:

'Seen some action, this bed, so they say . . .'

'Surprised it's still in one piece.'

'But what's she doing getting rid of it? She must be getting rid of it or why would she put it out here, eh? It's in good enough nick for a few more shags, I'd have thought.'

'There won't be much of that. He's buggered off. She's in despair. That's what I heard.'

'Yeah, but how long will that last, eh? Someone else'll come along and then what'll she do without a bed?'

'It's not the only one in the palace, bonehead.'

'No, but it's *the* bed. Right? It's, like, the *main* bed. The bed of beds.'

'What'll happen to it now? That's what I want to know. Who puts a bed in the middle of a courtyard? Ridiculous, that is. She could have done anything with it. Moved it to a guest room. Made a gift of it to a poor family. It'll get wrecked out here. Criminal waste, I call it.'

Cubby sat down on one of the stone benches that were set under the trees. He rubbed at his shoulder, which was going to have a massive bruise on it, for sure. He hadn't realized till that moment how sore it felt. Suddenly he became aware of someone standing behind him and he sprang to his feet. He knew it couldn't be one of the soldiers, for they were all down near the bed, laughing and talking, happy to have got shot of their burden. He turned and saw a woman leaning against one of the columns that rose from the marble floor to the roof of the colonnade. How could that be? Who was this? Cubby had never seen anyone half as beautiful in his life. Even the queen looked quite ordinary next to this lady. He gulped and shuffled his feet.

'Don't bother to speak, boy,' said this princess. She had to be at least a princess, Cubby reckoned. He had no intention of speaking, but he could see that the lady was crying. She was doing it very neatly. No bawling or red eyes for her, whoever she was. She just had a line of tears, like little pearls, creeping down her cheek. She lifted a corner of the flimsy-looking scarf she wore over her head and brushed them away.

'There! I've stopped crying now. There is no point in tears. Zeus has had his way again and that's all there is to it. Don't look so puzzled. You're too stupid to understand the ways of the Gods. I've spoken to you before – don't you remember? Never mind. You've clearly forgotten our last meeting. Dullards find it hard to keep any memory in their heads of the Gods they meet.'

'Gods? What're you on about?'

It occurred to Cubby that the woman might be drunk. Or mad. Who else would be wandering around the palace courtyard? But now that she mentioned it, she did look a bit familiar. He tried to think where he might have seen her before, and for a few moments something fluttered at the edge of his memory, but then it was gone and no matter how hard he racked his brains, he couldn't remember a thing. He decided not to worry about it.

'You have no idea who I am, have you?' she said. 'I'm Aphrodite, the Goddess of Love. My sister, Hera, and I fostered this love and now Zeus has sent his messenger, Hermes, to speak to Aeneas, and that's that. He's seen to it that it's all over. He's taken him away from her.'

'Who? Taken who away?'

'Fool! You're nothing but a dimwit. My son, Aeneas, and his men and ships will leave Carthage very soon and it's Zeus' doing. Dido is bereft. That's why she's given orders for the bed to be brought out here.'

What did *bereft* mean? Cubby had no idea but knew it couldn't be anything good from the way she said it. Perhaps it just meant that Dido would be sad because Aeneas was leaving. Everyone knew who he was. He'd been part of life at the palace for ages. Maron had explained on the very first day that his master was a prince who came from far away, from somewhere called Troy. You couldn't live here and not know that, but how come this creature who said she was a goddess also said she was his mother? She didn't look old enough to be anybody's mother. Cubby was feeling more confused than he usually did when people told him things, and that was saying something.

16

He asked, 'What's going to happen to it – to the bed?'

The lady came to sit next to him on the stone bench. He blinked. Perhaps, he thought, I'm asleep and this is my dream. There was a kind of music in the air as she moved, which came, he realized, from silver bells sewn on to the hem of her dress. He could smell her now too: a fragrance like roses and almond blossom. If I put out a hand, Cubby told himself, I could touch her scarf. He imagined how it would feel under his fingers, like mist or a stream of water, but pale green and pink and threaded with gold.

She shouted at him, right in his face: 'You're stupid and witless and shouldn't be here at all. This is wasted on the likes of you. Nothing good will come of it, you can be sure of that.'

Cubby blinked. When he opened his eyes, she'd gone. The beautiful lady was nowhere to be seen.

'You!' The master of the guard was shouting at him again. 'Back inside now. Look sharp. Plenty more to bring out here. This bed's just the start of it.'

Cubby plodded along behind the other men, frowning and trying to remember what she'd said her name was. Aphra-something. What else was there to bring out? What did that mean? When would he be getting back to the kitchen? He was starting to feel a bit sleepy and stared down at his feet as they covered the ground back to the bedrooms. One foot in front of the other. Suddenly it came to him where he'd seen her before. Aphrodite – that's her name, Cubby told himself, and felt quite clever for a change, because he'd remembered after all. It made him go red in the face just thinking about that day. He was glad the light was dim and was pretty sure the others, the real guards, hadn't noticed him blushing like a silly girl. He'd tried to put everything that had happened then out of his mind, because thinking about it made him feel confused and wobbly inside. Mostly he succeeded, but bits of what happened on the day he met Aphrodite sometimes came back to him, and then he felt a mixture of shame and a sort of longing for something he didn't quite understand. He tried to concentrate on what he was doing. He counted steps and tried to make a list in his head of all the bits and pieces he'd carried from various rooms to put on the bed, and soon the beautiful lady he'd met in the courtyard and everything she reminded him of had been pushed firmly to the back of his mind.

Elissa

Early morning; a palace corridor/a small bedchamber

The queen had hidden herself in a small room, right at the end of one of the longest corridors in the palace, and Elissa had been sitting just outside it on a wooden bench for what seemed like a very long time. Anna, the queen's sister, had told her to stay there just in case Dido wanted anything. Elissa was wondering if she could slip away for a while and go down to the harbour. How could she let Ascanius go without kissing him goodbye? Her eyes filled with tears as she imagined the boy being dragged on to the ship and begging his father, asking over and over, *Where's Elissa? I want Elissa* . . . She could hear his voice clear in her head, as though the child were beside her. She was so deep in thought that she didn't see Iopas till he was standing in front of her.

'Elissa? Are you all right? You seem to be . . . in some distress.'

'Thank you, Iopas,' Elissa answered, making an

effort to sound cheerful and strong. Iopas, according to Nezral and Tanith, was hiding a deep love for her, but as far as she could see, all he did was look at her searchingly from time to time. He never followed her, nor tried to make sure he stood next to her when the opportunity arose. He had never even spoken to her much, so perhaps her friends were exaggerating. They loved gossiping and Elissa didn't believe half the things they told her. But now, here he was, standing with his hands hovering in the air as though he wanted to stroke the top of her head and looking (Nezral's words for him) *all moony-eyed*. Elissa hoped very much that if she sounded firm and happier than she felt, he'd put his hands down by his sides again. He wasn't bad-looking: thin and tall with fairish hair and long eyelashes, but he didn't seem special in any way that she could see. Just lately, he seemed to spend most of his time following Dido or Anna about, making sure he didn't miss anything of interest that might turn into a poem, and most people in the palace thought he was nosier than he needed to be: always glad of any scraps of information or rumour that he might use. Some said he was cruel in the uses he made of his knowledge, but Elissa hadn't seen this unkindness for herself.

'D'you mind if I sit down and talk to you for a moment?' Iopas said, and Elissa nodded. I can hardly say no, she thought. He sat down next to her and went on: 'I'm still tired. I was woken up so early by the queen. Did you hear her? You must have. No one in the palace could have slept through her screams. It was terrifying. I thought at first it must be some wild creature – that was when I was still half asleep – but of course as soon as I raced out into the corridor I could see what it was. Poor Dido! My heart aches when I think of her sorrow. I don't think I've ever seen anyone so much in love. In fact' – he turned a little so that he was looking at Elissa – 'I was in the hunting party on the day they were married. That's what the queen called it. Have you heard that story, Elissa? Shall I tell you about it? I have the tale on good authority from Maron, who spoke to someone who was actually in the cave . . .'

That was another thing she'd heard about Iopas. He was boastful about his inside knowledge of the queen's household and liked telling stories he hoped would impress his listeners.

'Not now, Iopas,' she said. 'I'm not in the mood for stories. I'm sorry. I don't mean to be rude but I feel so sad. Both for the queen and for myself.'

'You? And why are you sad?'

Elissa was caught off-guard, wondering what to say, when Iopas struck his forehead with the heel of his hand and said, 'I'm a fool. Of course I know why you're sad. You're missing Ascanius. I'd noticed how fond of him you are. But why are you sitting here?'

Would he never stop his questioning? Elissa said, 'I'm waiting to see if the queen needs anything. You don't have to stay and keep me company, you know. I'll be perfectly all right on my own.' As soon as the words

21

were out of her mouth, Elissa regretted them. I sound churlish and ungrateful, she thought, and whatever I think of him, perhaps he *is* only being kind to me. She went on: 'I don't mean to be horrible, Iopas. I'm grateful for your sympathy, but I'm sure you have things to attend to.'

'Well,' Iopas said, standing up, 'there's always something waiting to be written. Some verse or other. Especially now. Perhaps the queen will require a lament for Aeneas' departure. I'll ask her when I see her. Be happy, Elissa.'

'Thank you, Iopas,' Elissa said, relieved to see him walking quickly away from her.

As he left, he passed Tanith, who was making her way towards Elissa along the corridor. She usually wore her dark, curly hair bound up in a scarf but today it hung over her shoulders, uncombed. When she reached the bench, she said, 'I've found you at last. What're you doing here?'

'Tanith! I'm not doing anything really. I was thinking of Ascanius and—'

'I'm not supposed to be here. There's yesterday's laundry to be done and the others will wonder where I am. But I've been looking for you everywhere. You're the only one who understands how miserable I am.'

It was true that Tanith, who almost always smiled a great deal, looked quite unlike herself. Her mouth was set in a straight line and she was pale and you could still see she'd been crying. She had come into Dido's service just before Elissa, and the two girls, together with Nezral, had shared a room and been friends since those days, more than four summers ago.

'Maron's gone,' Tanith said, sitting down beside Elissa on the bench and sighing. 'I'll never find someone like him again. No one else has ever paid me so much attention. No one has ever liked me in that way, but he did. Oh, the things he said to me! He spoke such beautiful words to me, and now when I remember them, I just want to cry.'

'I know, Tanith. It's a sad day for everyone. The queen herself is crying. I've heard her, sitting here, weeping like anyone else. And Maron was a lovely person and we'll miss him, but of course it's worst for you. But don't say you'll never find anyone else. Of course you will. Other young men will like you just as much.'

Tanith shook her head. 'No, Elissa. I'm not pretty like you, nor clever like Nezral, and Maron was the first person to notice me. In that way.'

Was she pretty? Elissa knew that her hair was glossy and dark; that her body was straight and quite tall; that her eyes were brown and flecked with green – but pretty? She'd never thought of herself as that. She changed the subject.

'Do you remember when we first met Maron? How he came into the room where we were playing with Ascanius and said, *You might not think I look much like a nursemaid but that's what I've been up till now.*'

Tanith smiled in spite of herself. 'Yes, I remember. He picked up a cloth lying over the linen chest and tied it round his head and walked about the room pretending to be a fat old nanny! And we couldn't help laughing. He knew how to do that – make everyone laugh. That was what Ascanius liked about him.'

The girls were silent for a moment, remembering Maron, who had come into the palace and immediately made friends with everyone. That was his gift. Elissa said, 'He liked people. He was happy to speak to anyone and treat them as a friend. Look at Cubby. No one ever speaks to him, do they? They think he's stupid and ignore him most of the time. I've always felt quite sorry for him, but I'd never dare to speak to him. I'd feel . . . I don't know. A bit strange, in case he didn't understand me properly, or something. Maron didn't think about things like that, though. I saw him quite often, chatting with Cubby in the kitchen. I expect Cubby's sad today too.'

'He doesn't look sad. They've got him standing guard by the bed in the courtyard. He looks the same as always. He doesn't feel as sad as I do, I'm sure. I can't stop myself from crying, Elissa.'

Elissa put an arm around her friend and Tanith wiped her eyes on a corner of her skirt. She said, 'I have to go. What are you doing now?'

'I have to stay here,' Elissa said. 'I'm supposed to wait here in case the queen needs anything.'

'Farewell then.' Tanith stood up and her mouth made the shape of a smile, but Elissa could see that her eyes were still sorrowful. She made her way towards the laundry, with her head bowed.

Just then, Dido called out from within her chamber. 'Elissa? Is that you?'

Elissa sprang up at once and went to the door. 'Yes, my lady,' she said, coming into the room. The light was dim and Elissa could tell that it would be in shadow till late afternoon. The queen sat on the narrow bed, which was one of only three pieces of furniture in the chamber. There was a small chair and a table under the window. The bed was spread with a coverlet made from the skins of wild animals, stitched together. Dido lifted one corner of it and smiled up at Elissa.

'You know the story about the ox hide, don't you, Elissa? Sit down, child. I don't want to be alone just now.'

Everyone knew the story, but Elissa didn't want to say anything to stop the queen from telling it again. If she was remembering the old days, when she was young, she'd be distracted from her sorrow. It might make her feel better. Elissa said, 'You were very young when you came to Carthage, I know.'

'But clever. Everyone still says how clever I was!' Dido smiled. 'The chieftains promised me that I could do what I liked with all the land that could be bounded by the skin of an ox. Silly creatures! They thought I meant an ox hide spread out over the earth.'

'But you tricked them!'

'It was easy. They all had their eyes hanging out, looking at me. It wasn't every day that a young widow on the run from her husband's murderer came to their attention. They all thought they wanted to help me, but the truth was they fancied themselves as suitors for my hand and couldn't understand that I didn't want any power through them. I wanted it for myself. On my own. And yes, I tricked them. I ordered my best and most skilful seamstress to cut the hide as though she were making a garment of softest cloth. Oh, you should have seen her! She had a glinting silvery-sharp knife and she traced its tip over the leather, slicing a thin border from the outer edge and then moving in a circle that grew smaller and smaller, till there was a long strip of leather, as narrow as a ribbon, lying on the ground. And when I laid it out, it stretched out so far that it took in most of the land on which the city now stands. The chieftains couldn't believe it.' Dido laughed, though there was little mirth in the sound. 'Well, that's not quite true, of course – it wasn't *that* long, but it took in so much more than they expected, and they were so stunned by my cheek that they agreed to give me everything: the land Carthage stands on and even more besides. And I allowed them to think that there might be hope for one of them as my husband . . . Too late for that now. I started work on building the city almost at once. And I asked for their help with stonemasons, carpenters and engineers, which made them happy. I paid well, of course. It's amazing, isn't it, how much a little gold greases the wheels.'

Elissa said, 'It was clever trick. Perhaps the chieftains admired your cleverness.'

'Yes,' Dido said, and went to stand at the window

with her back to Elissa. 'And I had my city. I did every-thing – I've done everything – to make it a fine city, and it *is* beautiful, isn't it?'

'Very beautiful,' Elissa said. 'Tall, fine buildings. Green gardens – rich farmlands outside the city too.'

'And yet I sometimes long for my country. I can't help it. The trees there – they aren't a bit like those we have here. I've planted cedars and vines, but they aren't quite at home in the landscape. A little like me. I still yearn for my childhood. My first husband. And sometimes I wish I didn't have to be a monarch all the time. You have no notion of how burdensome it is, ruling over a people. Never being able to lay that burden down because you have a duty to them; to your people – do you understand?'

Elissa nodded, though she didn't say what was in her mind. If Dido found being a queen so tiresome, why had she not sailed with Aeneas to wherever it was he was bound? Surely he must have asked her . . . No, the truth was, Dido loved being queen more than any-thing. She loved the power she had over the inhabitants of Carthage. She loved her own fame and reputation. She would never, never give up the pleasure of being a queen; the supreme ruler of her kingdom. How many times, Elissa thought, have I walked behind her as she processed through the city? Dido sometimes travelled on a kind of moving platform carried through the streets by six strong men from the palace guard, with Elissa and the other women walking alongside and behind her. The crowds stood on the edge of the roadway, and waved and cheered as she passed, and some of them even knelt down in the dirt and touched their foreheads to the ground, and Elissa felt a little of the thrill of being adored. Sometimes she could imagine that everyone was worshipping *her*, but that was just a foolish day-dream she indulged in to pass the time and she knew the truth of the matter. It was Dido, dressed in flowing robes of purple and red embroidered with fine gold threads, and with a headdress fashioned from beaten copper studded with opals on her head – she was the one the people loved; the one they admired and revered.

The queen went to lie on the bed, and Elissa was on the point of asking permission to return to her duties when she noticed a movement in the corner of the small room. She turned round and was startled to see someone standing in the shadows near the door.

'Dido, Queen of Carthage, is unhappy,' the some-one said, and when the visitor began to float towards the bed, not quite touching the floor, with the turquoise, silver-embroidered draperies of her robes shimmering and moving around her like smoke, Elissa wondered if this was a dream.

'Recognize Aphrodite, the Goddess of Love,' said the vision.

'Aphrodite!' Elissa gazed at her open-mouthed and couldn't think of what to say next.

'My poor child,' the Goddess said. 'Do not blame me for the queen's unhappiness. Nor for your own. As you know, all my desire is to foster love. Blame Zeus for Aeneas' departure. He's the one who sent Hermes to remind the Trojan of his duty.'

'Was it you who made her love Aeneas?' Elissa asked.

'Don't chide me,' Aphrodite whispered. 'What's done is done – nothing comes of mourning the past. And we Gods do not take kindly to being scolded. Everything that has to be will be, and all will become clearer as time passes.' She put an arm round Elissa, who was aware of the faintest touch, as though someone had wrapped a scarf of finest silk around her shoulders.

'Help her, Aphrodite,' Elissa said.

There was no answer. The Goddess had dissolved into the air, leaving behind a lingering fragrance of roses and almond blossom. Elissa opened her mouth to cry out again but her throat was dry. She turned to look at the queen, who had risen from her bed again and was staring out of the window. She stood with her head bowed and her back bent, leaning against the sill like an invalid. Shall I go and comfort her? Elissa wondered. She did that for me when I was sick.

Her mind returned to a time very soon after she'd arrived in the palace. Anna, the queen's sister, had arranged for Elissa to be one of the sewing women, and she was grateful because the work was pleasant and she would be spared the harshness of kitchen and laundry work. One day, as she was mending a tear in one of the palace draperies, Elissa's head began to swim and heat rose up into her face and all her limbs felt heavy and sore. It hurt to swallow. Her throat, it seemed to her, had turned into a thicket of spiky, thorny plants. She had pressed on with her stitching until at last she collapsed with her face on the draperies and Anna jumped up from her place at the top of the table.

'Elissa! Are you sick, my dear?'

Anna herself accompanied Elissa to the bed-chamber, which was empty because Tanith and Nezral were still at work. The queen's sister helped her undress and made her lie down under the coverlet and said: 'I'll send someone to you with a soothing drink, child. You must rest here till you are better.' She smiled. 'You are no use to me drooping over the table!'

Elissa dozed for a while and the dreams that filled her head were of her mother. Every time she woke and realized where she was and how far she was from her home, tears slipped out of the corners of her eyes and slid down on to her pillow. Every part of her hurt and she longed for her mother. I'm stupid, she told herself over and over again. If I was ill at home, I'd be in a crowded room with the little ones shouting and crying, and Ma would be busy and wouldn't have time to cuddle me or tend me or bring me soothing drinks.

'Elissa?' It was Dido herself, standing at the foot of her bed, and carrying a folded cloth in one hand and a bottle in the other. She put the bottle on the windowsill and sat down on the bed. 'I've brought you a damp cloth. Look – it's been wrung out in scented water and will cool your fever.'

She bent over Elissa and smoothed the wet cloth over her brow. A fragrance of jasmine rose in the air and the chill and the damp were delicious.

'Thank you, lady,' Elissa murmured. 'That's lovely. I feel much better, really. I'll soon be back at work.'

'No rush to do that,' said Dido. She ran her fingers over and over Elissa's brow in a soft, stroking motion and Elissa couldn't stop herself from crying. 'You must miss your mother,' the queen went on. 'And I wish I could be more motherly. I've never had the chance to learn, you see, but I'll look after you as best I can. Here, you must drink as much cool water as possible. Sit up, my child.'

Elissa struggled to sip out of the bottle. Dido's arm was now supporting her, and when Elissa had drunk her fill, she felt the queen lay her down again on the pillows. Before she left the room, she bent down and kissed Elissa's brow and said: 'Sleep now. You'll feel much better soon.'

And she had felt better the next day. Perhaps Dido had put some kind of healing draught into the water. From that time Elissa had always known that the queen cared for her, and she in turn loved Dido without reserve.

Surely now, she told herself, shaking the memories from her mind, I ought to be able to offer her some comfort? Elissa patted Dido gently, tentatively, on the shoulder. She knew that any words she could find would be of little help but she spoke nevertheless, trying to hide the trembling in her voice.

'I wish I could say something to make you feel better, lady. It makes me sad to see your sorrow.'

'I know that, Elissa. I know it and you're right. There's nothing to be done for me. You should go. You should leave me now.'

'Well . . .' Elissa hesitated. 'It's true that there's work to be done and I'll be missed by my companions.'

'Yes, child. Go. Send my sister to me.'

'I will,' said Elissa. 'I know she'll be worrying about you.'

She opened the door and stepped into the corridor, where bright sunshine striped the marble floor. It would be hot walking down to the harbour, but that couldn't be helped. She would go to her room and find a scarf to cover her head and tell Nezral or Tanith to make some excuse for her if Anna or anyone else wanted to know where she had gone.

Towards midday; the harbour

'Please, I beg you. You have to let me see him. I need to say . . . I need to tell him . . .' Elissa stared into the eyes of the Trojan barring her way. There were six of them, standing in a row, blocking the path to the shore. The men were lined up shoulder to shoulder, and she could no longer see what she'd glimpsed from the windows of the palace: Aeneas' men swarming near the moorings of their ships and preparing to leave, loading weapons and other possessions on to the decks. Now that she was here at the harbour, she could see that what she'd feared was true: he was already on board and determined to sail away, and the cries of the sailors sounded to Elissa like the songs of a thousand seabirds prophesying doom.

'Forget about it,' said one of the men. 'He's not allowing anyone through, much less a chit of a girl like you. He's given strict orders. We've got a tide to catch tomorrow, see, and no time to waste. All this gear to load. Go home, missy. You're not going to see him and that's that.'

'But you don't understand. I'm the nursemaid. I look after Ascanius. His son . . . I've been taking care of him the whole time he's been here. Please. I need to see my baby. I need to say goodbye. I implore you.'

'Nursemaid, eh?' The Trojan laughed and his companions joined in. 'Bit too young for that, and much too pretty, I'd say. And anyway, Ascanius is too big for a nurse. He's a boy, not a baby. Mind you' – the man nudged his elbow into his neighbour's side and laughed – 'wouldn't mind you being *my* nursemaid. Not a bit. Nice, that would be – right, lads? Nestling in that bosom.'

'You're disgusting!' Elissa said, but she muffled her words with her scarf. There was no chance of getting through this human barrier or of seeing Aeneas once more if she made them angry. She noticed something moving at the edge of her vision and turned to see who it was creeping up on her.

'Do you know who I am?' said the young man.

33

'You are Hermes, the messenger of the Gods,' she answered. 'You were in our room this morning.'

'Indeed,' Hermes said. 'Maron had to be brought down to the harbour.'

Elissa noticed the wings on Hermes' helmet, which made him seem more than ever like a woodland creature. His eyes, which she could see clearly now that she was close to him, were pale green and translucent. They reminded Elissa of the eyes of the orange-furred cats that came to hunt plump mice around the palace granaries. But Hermes' eyes had no darkness at their centres, and Elissa shivered and found it impossible to look straight at him. She bent her head and fixed her gaze on his heels, where a second pair of gold-edged wings trembled in the slight breeze blowing in from the sea.

'It's time for Aeneas to fulfil his destiny. He has to leave at once, or he will stay here for ever. And that is not in the plan the Gods have outlined. Don't cry, though. It's really nothing personal.'

Hermes' voice sounded high and girlish but it held a thread of menace and Elissa didn't dare to say what she really wanted to say, which was: *It's personal to me.* A god wouldn't understand mortal grief or pain.

'You're wrong,' said Hermes. 'We know exactly how hard it is to part from a loved one. We know how weak mortals are and how little defence they have against pain. We grieve for you all.'

'I didn't say anything,' Elissa cried.

'You didn't need to. I could read your mind.'

Hermes laughed. 'It's not hard, in your case, to work out how you feel. You are a picture of unhappiness – and of course I know why.'

'If you can't help me to see Aeneas, then I wish you'd go away. It's upsetting to hear this. I don't care about his destiny. I just wish—'

'Your wishes are of no consequence to the Gods, Elissa,' Hermes said, rising a little way off the ground and beginning to move back towards the harbour. 'You are not part of Aeneas' story and that's all there is to it.'

'He could have said goodbye to me,' Elissa cried. 'How difficult would that have been?'

Hermes shook his head and his helmet-wings flapped a little. 'Take heart, girl,' he said. 'You have duties to the queen. She will depend on you, you know. You do have a part to play in this drama. You will find out later . . .'

He was too far away by now to speak to, but if she could, Elissa would have shouted after him: *It's not a drama. It's my life.* She sighed and continued staring at the ships, peering into the distance, trying to spot Aeneas or Ascanius, but there was no sign of them.

In spite of Hermes' words, Elissa was still both furious and sad. She sat down on a pile of stones left behind by builders who had recently been improving the houses around the harbour. Aeneas had gone without so much as a word to her and she was left carrying the burden of her love for him and unable to speak of it to anyone. She had hidden this love so well and for so long and from so many people that covering up how she felt had become second nature to her, but today the truth was pressing to come out, to be told to everyone, and still she couldn't say a word. She was sad about Ascanius. That was the story they all believed.

As long as Aeneas was still here, she told herself, I could hope for something. How many hours had she dreamed away, imagining the two of them together, like husband and wife, with Ascanius playing at their feet? Even during their brief, rare times together she'd been lost in daydreams of his face, how handsome he was, and she could think of nothing except how he made her feel when he looked at her, and when he touched her. Whenever he spoke to her, she was so taken up with admiring the beauty of his mouth that she hadn't paid very much attention to what he said, but it was true that he had promised her nothing. Still, she couldn't help herself. She didn't know how to stop hoping for something miraculous, something impossible, and she offered prayers to Aphrodite every night.

And what would become of Dido now? she wondered. Whatever energy had been left over from her own longing for Aeneas was filled with agonies of jealousy, because he loved the queen and she adored him. But I love the queen too, Elissa thought, and would never wish to hurt her, and what I've done would hurt her if she ever found out about it. These feelings were like bad stomach ache, but worse than the worst pain she'd ever suffered. If Aeneas left now, would the jealousy disappear simply because Dido had also been abandoned? And could she be in the queen's presence without flushing red with embarrassment?

I should have spoken to him earlier, Elissa told herself, while he was still here to speak to. Why didn't I dare to tell him how much I loved him? Because I'm too young. Every time he was with me I was tongue-tied. Dazzled by love. In awe of him because he was a hero and I am no one. A servant. His son's nursemaid. And on that night (nearly three moons ago, but Elissa turned it over in her mind all the time, every single day, because it was so extraordinary, like a bright jewel shining in her heart), I could have told him how much I loved him, but I didn't want to say a word that might have warned him he was making a mistake. I wish, she said to herself, I wish I had that night back again. Wishing, she knew, was useless.

Now she wondered why Aeneas had said nothing to her, not even a word of farewell. Even as she was thinking this, a truth came to her. His flight had nothing to do with her and he didn't think of her as someone from whom he ought to take his leave. She was no more than the girl who looked after Ascanius, and even if there was that one night – a night which she'd thought would make it possible for her to be more to him than that – it had been quite clear for some time that Aeneas regretted what had passed between them. She had noticed that he'd been avoiding her, and now he was leaving Carthage for reasons which she was ignorant of and probably wouldn't understand, but which had nothing whatsoever to do with her. Elissa shivered and thought of Aphrodite ... Aeneas had often spoken of her.

'She's my mother, Elissa,' he'd said once, and she'd wondered how that could be. How could a mortal be the son of a goddess? She was about to ask him when he continued: 'It's all been decided by the Gods, you see. There's little we can do when they've made up their minds. My mother and Hera looked with favour on Dido's love for me and allowed it to flourish but I've always . . .'

'Always what?' Elissa dared to ask. Sometimes when Aeneas came into the nursery and stayed to talk to her, she found it hard to find words, even though she longed for the conversation to continue, but on this occasion her curiosity gave her courage.

Aeneas had smiled at her. His whole face changed when he smiled and he looked more like his little son and less like a warrior. If something angered him, his eyes, the look that came into them, could make you feel cold all over. He said, 'I've always known that the Gods had something prepared for me. Call it a sense of – what's the right word? Destiny. Yes, that's it. D'you know what that means, Elissa?'

She'd shaken her head. Aeneas continued: 'It's hard to explain, only I've always known that I was spared during the war in Troy because there was something else I had to do before I died. And now it's clear. I am to found a new city across the sea.'

'Does that mean you're leaving us?' she had

asked him. 'Can you not be a lord here, in Carthage?'

'Oh, Elissa, it's complicated. Queen Dido would be reluctant to share her power, I think.'

'Have you asked her?' Even as she spoke, she realized that he might well chide her for her words. As a mere nursemaid, she knew she had no right to ask for details about the affairs of her masters.

'Whatever she says now, she would grow to hate it, as you know. And besides, it's as I said. No one can escape the fate which the Gods have decreed.'

Elissa used to love these talks, even though after a while she grew a little bored with discussions of destiny, but it appeared that whatever it was, this *destiny* was the cause of her sorrow: the one thing that made it impossible for Aeneas to remain in Carthage.

She stood up and looked around. Could she duck past the soldiers; make a run for the ships? No, of course she couldn't. The men (who weren't really soldiers but looked and behaved and strutted around like soldiers and regarded themselves as Aeneas' bodyguard) would catch her. Stop her. They'd send her back to the palace, and if the queen found out that she'd been down here wanting to see Aeneas . . . Elissa shivered. Perhaps Dido would banish her. Send her back home. This would certainly be the worst fate she could imagine, for however much she loved Aeneas, she loved Dido too, and to leave her service would be a kind of a death. Her father would punish her for what she'd done when she was only a girl, running away from his house. Now, more than four summers later, Elissa thanked the Gods every day that she was here, in Carthage, serving a beautiful queen and living in a palace that was a wonder of the world.

She started to cry as she turned away from the harbour and began to walk back to the palace, and the tears flowed from her eyes as though they would never stop. No, she told herself. I'll keep silent. Say nothing. Aeneas will forget about me. I was nothing to him. He was everything to me. All my prayers to Aphrodite have come to nothing. How she wished that tomorrow she could wake up to find Ascanius standing over her bed almost as soon as the sun was up, saying: *Playtime, Elissa. Get up now, Elissa*, as he did every day. But the boy was leaving with his father and the two of them would never come back. He'd have Maron to take care of him now, but surely, surely he'd miss her? Maron was more like a boisterous elder brother to the boy, but she . . . she felt herself to be a kind of mother to Ascanius. She sobbed into her scarf. She could tell that her eyes (*Oh, Elissa, I could drown in your eyes* – that was what he'd said to her, that night) would by now be rimmed with scarlet and bloodshot and surrounded by puffy flesh. She touched her eyelids and of course they were disgustingly swollen after so many tears but still she couldn't stop crying.

She made her way back through the silent streets. The sun was lower in the sky now, and in the market-place she could hear the stallholders talking and laughing among themselves as they cleared up the mess left after a morning's trading. A scattering of squashed fruit and vegetables was all that remained of the fresh produce that the farmers had brought from the terraces west of the city. Everything good had been sold early in the day, before the sun was at its highest, and now only the worst quality produce remained: flabby-looking fish, bruised fruit and fatty meat. Elissa sat down on a bench near the flower stalls, suddenly feeling sick. She'd been feeling ill on and off for a few days, and wondered how soon she'd be well again. Taking two or three deep breaths, she tried to calm herself. How different, she thought, my life would have been if I'd never come to Carthage and to Dido's glorious palace.

The queen had been kind to her from the very first time they'd met, and part of Elissa's present anguish sprang from that. How beautiful she was when she spoke to me, Elissa thought, on that day four summers ago! Her hair, like burnished copper, was bound up and plaited with silver threads, but Elissa knew that it would spring into waves and ringlets the moment it was untied, set free. Dido's skin was like ivory and her eyes like dark green glass when you held it up to the sun: a deep, rich colour but full of light.

Someone from the palace guard had brought her into the great hall and pushed her to her knees in front of the queen.

'We found her hiding behind the stables, lady,' he said. 'She says she's run away from home. Can't be more than twelve summers old, I'd say.'

'Stand up, child. What's your name?'

'Elissa, lady. And I'm not a child. I was twelve three moons ago.'

The queen smiled, and Elissa remembered how she'd felt at the time: as though she'd been cold and uncomfortable and was suddenly in the warmth again, as though the sun were shining on her.

'How strange,' she said, 'that we are both named Elissa, even though I have chosen to call myself Dido. *Elissa* was the name I was given at birth and it reminds me of another life, another time, when I was happy and young and living with a husband who loved me.'

Those were the queen's first words to me, Elissa thought, and since then there's been something between us: some connection. I didn't say very much when she spoke to me that first day. I was too shy, too scared. But I knew the story of how she'd come to Carthage. Everyone, even in our village, high up in the mountains, knew how the city had been founded.

Dido's – Elissa's – husband, Sychaeus, had been killed – murdered by her own brother. This wicked man wanted Sychaeus' gold and treasure for himself, and was quite ready to kill his own sister to get it, but the ghost of Sychaeus appeared to Dido in a dream and warned her, telling her where the treasure was hidden. She fled by night on ships laden with gold and jewels, accompanied by her sister, Anna, and many followers. And now, even though she had created the city of Carthage, which was a wonder among the rulers of the surrounding lands, Elissa knew she yearned for Tyre, her real home. Before Aeneas arrived she was sad for the loss of the man she loved and always aware that she had the duties of a monarch to fulfil. She had to act in every way so as to further the interests of her new city and make it as strong in the region as all the other states that surrounded it. Stronger, even. Then the Trojan sailed into the harbour and everything changed.

Elissa knew nothing about being a queen, but she recognized the need for strength. There had been times, on the road from her home to the coast, when her courage had almost failed her. She'd left her father's house at dawn one day, carrying nothing more than a bundle of clothes and some stolen bread. She was the eldest child of five, born to a mother who loved her but spent so much of every day cleaning, cooking, tending the smaller children and working to placate her husband that she was like a cloth soaked and wrung out too many times. Elissa and her younger sisters and brothers did what they could to help her, but it was not enough. There was the land they owned – not much of it – to be ploughed and sown with seed, and then the harvest to be gathered and stored and sold in the market. And poor Ma had to help with that as well, Elissa reflected, so it was no wonder she had no time to care for us, to shield us. Worst of all, her father had plans for her to marry. He'd chosen a monster called Shillek. Elissa recalled his slack, loose lips which he licked constantly, leaving them coated with a kind of horrible gloss; his unthinking cruelty to small animals and children: all he could talk about was

43

hunting – what he'd killed today and what he hoped to kill tomorrow. He thought his skill with the spear made him a hero, but to Elissa, even though she knew the community depended on its hunters for food, this made him boring as well as cruel, and very ugly. Why should animals die a bloody death to put food into the mouths of brutal young men? She ate the meat along with everyone else, but dwelling on how it came to her plate disgusted her. Just thinking about Shillek and that meat now was making her feel ill again.

She stood up, thinking: I'll go and find Tanith and Nezral. They're my friends and we're used to one another. It didn't matter that Nezral had a sharp tongue, nor that Tanith was sometimes absent-minded and forgetful and lost in her own world. They talked about everything with one another and shared their most secret thoughts. They'll try and comfort me, she thought. I wish I didn't feel so ill.

Anna

Sometime after midday; a small bedchamber

'Please, Sister. Please listen. You'll make yourself ill if you don't eat. If you don't stop weeping. You haven't touched anything all day long. Here, take a morsel. A mouthful only.'

Dido was lying as still as a corpse on the bed. Her eyes were closed.

Anna said: 'I can see you want me to stop talking. I'm the chatterbox, I know it, and you're the quiet one. That's how it's been all our lives, hasn't it? People used to say it aloud when we were girls, and nothing has changed.'

'If you know so much, how is it you're still making such a racket? When you can see that I'm— my head aches and your voice isn't helping. You can't bear silence, can you? Isn't that true? And silence is what I need. What I crave. You've known me your whole life and you don't understand anything. I want to be on my own. I don't need you to look after me.'

'But look, Dido – at last you're speaking to me. I

thought you might never stop weeping, you know. Is that possible? Could someone weep for ever, d'you think? Anyway, I'm glad you've calmed down a little. We can talk of other things. And I don't care if you *are* angry with me. That's fine. I'm happy to see that you're beginning to sound a little more like yourself. If you're yelling at me, you can't be as sad as you were.'

Dido sat up, and even though Anna had heard some of her elder sister's displeasure in the words she spoke, she hadn't understood till that moment the full extent of her fury. It's her eyes, she thought. Why can't she have eyes that stay the same colour, like those of almost everyone else in the world? Dido's are sometimes green and sometimes blue, but when she's angry they flash a kind of turquoise fire. And her hair – well, it wasn't fair to judge that now, when she'd spent hours thrashing about on that ridiculous bed and hadn't changed her garments since she retired last night. It was a mess, standing out around her head like a fiery cloud. What colour was Dido's hair? No one, Anna reflected, is in any doubt about what colour mine is. It's brown. I have dark, shiny brown hair which falls straight to my shoulders and which men – some men – have admired, but anyone who sees Dido's hair for the first time is entranced, amazed; they can't quite believe the glory of gold and red that springs from her head and falls over her shoulders like a fiery waterfall.

'Oh, the rubbish you talk, Anna! Why would I feel less sad than I did an hour ago? I spoke to you because there was something I wanted to say. I wanted to tell you to go. Leave me alone.'

'I'm not going,' said Anna, and she sat down on the end of the bed.

Dido sighed loudly, turned over and buried her face in the pillows. 'But I want you to. I don't want to speak to anyone.' Her voice was muffled and Anna leaned forward, straining to hear the words.

'I don't care what you want. I'm staying. You don't have to say anything. I'll speak to you. I'll do what we used to do when we were girls, remember? We'd tell one another stories. I was good at it.'

'Not so good that I want to hear another of your tales now. You don't understand.' Dido had turned round again and sat up. 'I don't want to be distracted from my pain. You want me to think about something else and I refuse to. I want to think only about him. About Aeneas. I want to remember everything. D'you recall how he came to the court? I must have been crazed to allow that rabble of Trojans to land here. They looked like what they were: refugees. I ought to have pushed the whole lot of them back on to their patched-up ships and left them to fend for themselves on the ocean. They'd have drowned or been murdered by pirates and I'd have been spared all this.'

'You couldn't have done it. You're too kind.'

'And much good it did me. I was stupid. Taken in by a handsome face and a hard-luck story.'

'You had so much in common with him. Of course you were sympathetic. You, too, had fled your home and your country and everything you knew. And you were curious. Admit it. We'd heard such stories of the war in Troy, and there he was, straight from Priam's palace, and right on our doorstep. How could you possibly have turned him away? What a day that was! I remember everything about it.'

Anna was sitting in the courtyard of the new palace with Iopas, the young man whom Dido had recently appointed as court poet and singer. Part of her was uneasy. Would a person who wasn't a servant – never that – but perhaps not quite high enough in the court hierarchy to be a courtier be considered a suitable companion for the queen's younger sister? There's also the matter of his age, she told herself. He's younger than I am, though it's hard to guess by how much. If he is eighteen, then I'm nearly ten years older than he is. And I know nothing about him. He didn't seem like a married man, but you couldn't tell just by looking. At least, she thought, he's grateful to me. It's thanks to me Dido chose him. She would have gone for someone dignified and grey-haired, but I pointed out to her that only youth had the passion and fire to create poems and songs that would do credit to Carthage. 'We're a young city,' Anna told her sister. 'We need a young court singer. And look at him, Dido. He'll be an asset to us, truly.'

Dido had smiled. 'I can see *you* admire him, Anna,' she said. 'Very well, for your sake . . .'

Anna looked at Iopas and decided not to worry

about his age until she had to. Still, here was the perfect opportunity to find out a little more about this enigmatic young man. He was skinny, and not exactly handsome in any traditional sense, but his eyes were kind and fringed with long dark lashes, and there was a sweetness about his smile, when he did smile, that made Anna feel as if she wanted to put out a hand and stroke his smooth light-brown hair. She said, 'Are your parents alive?'

'No, they're both dead. My father used to have a small shop in the city, and died only five years ago, but I never knew my mother. She didn't live very long after I was born.'

'That must be a sadness for you. Have you always written poems? Sung songs? My sister was especially impressed with your playing of the lyre. She plays a little herself, you know.'

Iopas nodded and blushed. 'I find it easier to write and sing than to talk. I can be someone different from my real self then. And bringing music out of those instruments . . . it makes me feel' – he paused and smiled at Anna – 'powerful.'

'That must be wonderful indeed, but is being your true self so difficult?'

Iopas took some time to answer. 'No, not difficult, but the person I really am isn't . . . well, he isn't the heroic, brave, confident and eloquent person I'd like to be, so it's just as well I'm allowed to pretend as often as I like to be another sort of person altogether.'

'Well,' said Anna, 'you're still very young and might

well become all those things – heroic, brave, confident and so forth – when you're a little older, don't you think?'

I'm flirting with him, she thought. But Dido isn't here to chide me and Iopas is so pleasant and he likes me. I know he does. If matters progress, there will be time enough then to speak to my sister. Anna knew that Dido was ceaselessly conscious of station and rank and dignity; and she'd made quite certain from the very beginning of their time in Carthage that everyone knew that she was in control; that her word was law. That she was to be obeyed. Anna was almost sure that this applied to her as much as to anyone else and wondered sometimes about how her sister saw the world. Dido was clear that she ranked higher than most men, but they, of course, found this attitude strange and uncomfortable. Once, she'd even asked Dido about it, and she, who went through her life seemingly with no doubts about anything, had answered: 'It's my kingdom, Anna. I've been given this land. Fairly. It's mine. And I intend to make the city great. A force in the world. Everyone will wonder at it. And at me.'

Dido had wasted no time. She'd had the local chieftains in the palm of her hand. They were all besotted with her and some of them must have thought she would make them a good wife. They'd talked to their own builders and farmers and carpenters and engineers, and soon a whole army of workers was labouring to create this city that had sprung up on the shores of the ocean. Also, Anna reflected, Iarbas helped us. This man, a chieftain from the neighbouring territory, had been eager from the first to assist the young woman who'd suddenly found herself so powerful. He, like some of the others, had hoped Dido would be grateful and marry him, but there had never been any sign of her doing so, and Anna wondered how dangerous that was. He was the most persistent of the suitors. When they first came to Carthage, Dido pleaded promises made to Sychaeus. Iarbas was not repulsive to look at, even though he was no great beauty: a big ox of a man with twinkling blue eyes and a hearty laugh. He was friendly for the moment, but he could just as easily turn from a friend into an enemy, and that would be difficult. How would Carthage survive if it was surrounded on all sides by its enemies, by people who wanted nothing more than to take Dido's kingdom for themselves, by force if necessary?

And when we first came here, we were refugees ourselves and on the run, Anna thought. Poor Sychaeus! To this day she wished that she had paid proper attention to what she had seen only moments before his death, but there hadn't been time. It had all happened too quickly.

She'd been sewing, as she often did during the long afternoons, in the gardens of Sychaeus' palace in Tyre. The cedar tree that grew in the palace garden sheltered her from the worst heat of the sun. Her head was bent over her work, and suddenly she became aware that a shadow deeper than the shade of the tree had fallen over the fabric in her hands. She turned at once and jumped to her feet when she saw that a man was standing behind her.

'Who are you? How did you get past the guards at the gate?'

She felt suddenly icy cold and thought: I'm frightened. That's why I can't feel the heat of the sun any more. The man was tall – taller than anyone she'd seen before – and he wore a grey cloak even though this was the height of summer. He had a pale face, half hidden by the hood of his garment. When he spoke, his words came to her ears as though he were standing a long way away, and yet she could have put out a hand and touched him.

'I am Hades, the God of the Underworld. Of Death. I have come to warn you.'

'Warn me? Warn me of what?' Anna trembled, terrified.

'You will see. I must go to the appointed place.'

She watched the grey figure striding away and stood rooted to the spot, unable to move for what seemed like an eternity. When she recovered, when she found the strength to move again, she ran into the palace and found her sister, Dido, lying on the ground near the butchered body of her husband, weeping uncontrollably, the hem of her garment stained with the blood that pooled round Sychaeus' lifeless corpse. Their own brother had killed him. Of Hades there was no sign, and yet the day was no longer warm and sunny. A shadow had fallen over everything and Anna could tell that the God was still somewhere near them, hidden, waiting.

She shivered as she sat beside Iopas. To this day it hurt her to remember how brutally Sychaeus had been murdered. Dido didn't even have time to mourn him properly, because their murdering brother would have killed them too if they'd stayed. We had to flee, she thought, but thanks to Dido's cleverness we didn't go empty-handed. She'd always sworn to Anna that the hiding place for Sychaeus' treasure was revealed to her in a dream, but Anna thought it was much more likely that her sister had known where the gold was hidden even during her husband's lifetime. She shivered when she recalled how terrified and desperate she'd been when they arrived on this beautiful shore. Dido, Anna thought, had never seemed frightened, but then she'd always been the brave one; I'm the one who jumped at every shadow.

But Anna was also good at putting painful memories to one side. She turned to Iopas and said: 'Isn't it beautiful here? Hasn't my sister shown herself to be the best of queens?' Gardeners had only just finished planting palm trees in large white pottery tubs, decorated with dark blue snakes and dragons. Dido had ensured that the courtyards were almost the first things to be completed, once the living quarters and kitchens were ready. 'She loves flowers and trees and everything growing,' Anna explained, 'and these courtyards are like small gardens, aren't they?'

'Tamed gardens,' Iopas said. 'Not wildernesses.'

Anna looked at him and smiled. 'Who would want to create a wilderness?'

Iopas opened his mouth, perhaps to persuade her of how beautiful a desert could be, but at that moment a messenger raced into the courtyard, panting and sweating as though he'd run for a long time.

'Queen Dido. I have to speak to her. The harbour master has seen some ships making for our shores.'

Anna stood up. 'Follow me,' she said, and began to walk swiftly along the corridors leading to the great hall, which was where Dido was generally to be found at this time of day, poring over maps and plans of buildings going up in the city, or talking to her advisers – and sure enough, when she entered the room, she could see her sister sitting at a table with scrolls of parchment piled up around her. Various men Anna didn't recognize were standing about, waiting to hear what the queen was going to say.

'Dido,' she cried. 'A messenger is here. From the harbour master.'

'Madam . . .' The young man was now so out of breath that it took him a little while to collect himself. During those moments Dido sat very still and stared at him without saying a word.

'Madam, there are ships approaching the harbour. We've seen three but there may be others. We cannot see what kind of ship clearly yet, but the harbour master needs your instructions.'

Dido stood up. 'I think we should go down to the

harbour and see who these strangers are,' she said, gathering her robes about her and waving a hand to dismiss everyone else in the room. Anna watched as they gathered up the papers that had been spread out over the table and melted away almost before Dido had swept from the room. Anna followed her sister, almost running to keep up with her.

Outside the palace, the sun was striking the bright, clean stones of the new buildings and making them glitter. It was hot. Not unbearably so, but still Anna put on her headscarf to keep off the worst of the glare. Dido walked bareheaded, even though her skin was pale and burned easily. She could do this because a servant (whose duty it was to sit waiting, all day sometimes, in case the queen took it into her head to walk about the city) kept pace beside her, carrying a kind of awning on a stick which he held over her head so that she remained always in the shade. This arrangement also means that my sister can show off her hair, Anna reflected. Today, it was intricately braided and entwined with silver threads and hung down almost to her waist. Dido intended as many of Carthage's citizens as possible to see it – and they would, because somehow word had spread, even though this was a private excursion and not an official procession, and people were streaming down from houses on the hills, from shops, marketplaces and the temples built to the Gods, from inns and taverns near the harbour, all eager to see who had set their sails for land and was making for their shore.

'Queen Dido,' said the harbour master, a sleek, plump, middle-aged man, who had the manner of a host welcoming guests to a private party. 'What an honour to see you here! Come and sit in my quarters, madam, and stay out of this fierce sun.'

'I carry, as you see, my own shade with me,' Dido answered him, adding, perhaps conscious that this sounded ungracious: 'But thank you for your kindness and hospitality. Are we any clearer who's aboard these ships?'

'No, madam. It's hard to tell, but soon they'll be close enough for us to observe them properly.'

In the event, no one could believe what they were seeing from the harbour master's window when the three ships weighed anchor in the bay. They looked like vessels from a nightmare, their sails torn and ragged, the paint worn from their sides, and their figureheads broken and disfigured. Everyone was shouting and talking at once and some of what they said floated up like ribbons of words to where Anna and Dido were standing: 'Look – someone's coming ashore in a boat . . . haven't seen a bath in some weeks . . . Are they pirates? . . . No, the pirates've chased them here, looks like. How many? Can't tell . . . One of them's got a bandage round his arm . . . bleeding . . . Here they are . . . taking them to the harbour master . . . friends or enemies?'

Anna watched some sailors (sent, no doubt, by the harbour master himself) standing by as the small boat came close to the jetty; they jumped down into it and grabbed hold of the three occupants. She couldn't hear what they were saying to one another, but the strangers were led up very quickly – bundled up, you could almost say – to where she and Dido were standing. The harbour master huffed and puffed as he approached them.

'Now then, now then . . .' he said. 'What do we have here? Who are you and where do you come from?'

Of the three men who stood before them, one was clearly the leader. Another was an elderly, grizzled sailor and the third was very young. No more than a boy really, with reddish hair and a wide smile, full of energy and seemingly quite undaunted by his adventures on the ocean.

'We're grateful for your kindness,' said the leader. 'We've come a very long way and we've been travelling for many moons. We're Trojans who fled the city as it burned. You've heard tell of the war?'

Dido stepped forward then. Anna stared at the man and tried not to appear too astonished. His voice . . . Who in the realm of men had ever had a speaking voice like this? Perhaps he was Apollo in disguise. Didn't the Gods sometimes visit mortals without revealing their true identity? That was what the stories said, and this voice was beautiful. It was deep and true, and every word came to Anna's ears like a note of music made by a golden instrument. Although he was dirty, ragged and unkempt after a long sea voyage, he towered over the harbour master and it was hard not to admire his muscled, sun-browned arms. His hair and eyes were dark, and his nose as well-formed as that on a statue.

'You are welcome,' Dido said. 'I am Dido, Queen of Carthage.'

'An honour, madam,' he answered, and bowed very low. 'I am Aeneas, son of Anchises, of the city of Troy. This is my ship's captain, and that young scoundrel is Maron, who helps me with the care of my little son, Ascanius.'

She said, 'How many are you, on those ships?'

'There are thirty of us, madam. I've recently buried my poor father on the island of Sicily, but my son is thankfully still with me. I'm grateful to you for your kindness.'

'It's my pleasure. Go to your men and tell them they are welcome. We will return to our palace and prepare for your arrival. I am sorry to hear of your father's death. Harbour master, help Aeneas and his men to disembark in good order. We'll deal with the ships later. They seem to be in need of some repairs.'

'Pirates from the islands.' Aeneas smiled for the first time. 'They didn't kill us, but the fight was fierce and our poor ships suffered greatly.'

Dido returned his smile. 'We'll wait to greet you at the palace in due course. Baths and clothes will be prepared for everyone.'

Anna recalled how they'd left the harbour master's quarters then. Dido walked swiftly back up the hill, dismissing the awning-carrier with a wave of her hand.

'Anna,' she said, over her shoulder, 'may I leave this to you?'

'Of course. I'll be happy to organize everything.'

That was true, Anna thought. I like nothing better than seeing that households run like clockwork. As she struggled up the hill to the palace – the heat was terrible now – she considered what needed to be done. Servants summoned. The bathhouse cleared and fresh water drawn from the wells and brought to the palace and then heated. Clothes prepared – the palace guards would have to donate spare uniforms if there were thirty men to be clothed. For Aeneas himself, a chieftain would have to be asked to contribute some suitable garment, or perhaps she might ask some of the architects, counsellors and hangers-on who always thronged the corridors of the palace. And there was a child. It was important to find the right person to look after this boy, who was probably confused and frightened and missing his mother. That pleasant-looking lad Maron would have done his best, but young children needed women to take care of them. Who had his mother been? Anna wondered – but this wasn't the moment to become curious about this visitor's life. There would be time enough to find out such details later.

Dido turned to Anna as they reached the courtyard. 'A banquet tomorrow, Anna. It's much too late today, but we'll have a splendid banquet tomorrow. Show these Trojans how we live in Carthage. Can that be arranged?'

'Certainly,' Anna said, thinking: It'll be hard. I'll have to send at least a dozen people down to the market at first light. Warn them in the kitchens. Make sure the gold platters are polished, and the goblets too. 'I'll discuss food with the cooks. Boar? Lamb?'

'Both of those, but also, I think, peacock, if you can find it. It's so pretty when the cooks dress the birds with their own feathers. Anna . . . do you see that man? Over there. He's been following us up from the harbour. How can he wear such a long enveloping cloak in this heat?'

Anna turned and looked around. The description was exact. Hades was here . . . Where was he? She tried to sound unworried but she could feel dread gripping her, freezing her as it had on the day Sychaeus was murdered.

'Where? I don't see anyone. What colour cloak? You're imagining things.'

'Don't be silly.' Dido had stopped in the middle of the path and stood quite still. She spoke slowly, as if she were in a dream-state. 'Grey. A grey cloak. I'm not in the habit of imagining strange men. He's so tall, Anna. You must see him. There, just in the shadow of the wall.'

'No, I'm sorry. Perhaps it's a mirage.'

What did it mean – that Dido could see Hades and she could not? Could it be that her sister was in danger? She offered up a prayer to Hera, the sister of Zeus.

'Never mind,' Dido sighed. 'He's gone. I don't know

how or why but it's too hot to worry about him, whoever he was. What were we talking about?'

'The banquet. I said I'd try to find peacock,' Anna
said, trying to keep her voice steady. 'I can't promise
anything. Not with so little time.'

'Well, if anyone can do it, you can. And do come and
consult about my robes for the banquet when you've
finished dealing with everything else.'

Not a word of thanks, Anna reflected. Does she
realize what she sounds like? She shook her head. I'm
used to it. She's simply like that. She doesn't mean anything bad by such behaviour. She thinks of me as a sort
of extension of herself, and who in the whole universe
ever thanked themselves? No one, that's who.

Anna went to find Elissa, who, she thought, might be
a perfect nursemaid for the little boy. She wasn't much
more than a child herself, but kind and loving, and
also sensible and a favourite with Dido. At least
Aeneas' son would have the very best of care.

Mid afternoon; a small bedchamber

Anna allowed herself to drift back to the present and
leave behind her memories of Aeneas' arrival. She
could see, through the small window, a patch of
darkening sky, but still the afternoon light shone gold
over the harbour. There wasn't a sound to be heard,
and she wondered briefly where everyone was. They're
hiding, she told herself. Waiting to see how the

61

queen reacts. Perhaps the servants are eating in the kitchen. She was quite sure that everyone in the palace was there somewhere, waiting, because they were all obviously aware of Dido's anguish and would be eager to see what she needed; what she would do next. But no one, it seemed, had walked down the corridors for a long time and Anna decided that when she left her sister, the first thing she'd do was go and check that the sentries were still in their positions. This would be a good time for enemies to creep in and take over the palace. Iarbas wasn't exactly an enemy, of course, but jealousy made men act strangely, and he'd certainly had his eye on Dido ever since they came to Carthage. His nose was out of joint and no one likes that. Ever since it had become generally known in the city that Dido was in love with Aeneas, he'd been sulky, but who knew what effect the news of his rival's departure would have on him? Even though Dido had made it clear to him, long before Aeneas' arrival, that she had no intention of ever marrying him, men quite often didn't believe what they didn't want to believe and it was possible that he still held out some hope, especially now that his rival was leaving Carthage. Much better to make sure that the soldiers knew their duty and were constantly on guard against intruders.

Anna looked at Dido (who was not asleep, but lying very still on her back with one arm flung over her eyes) and said: 'Did you fall in love with Aeneas from the very first time we saw him? Looking filthy and ragged and unshaven?'

'Of course not. Why do you keep going on and on about that time? It's past and won't return.'

'Well, you refuse to speak to me, so what choice do I have? I must think about something.'

Dido gave a scornful laugh. 'And that's the best you can do? I can't imagine anything more boring.'

'How can you say that, Dido? The feast we laid on is still talked about. We've never had such a magnificent occasion here at the palace, either before or since. Iopas singing all the songs of welcome – how nervous he was beforehand: d'you remember? It was his first public appearance as court singer and his hands were shaking. Then Aeneas' stories. I know very well you remember those. Which of us had heard such things before? And his voice—'

'Not another word about his voice!' Dido sobbed. 'It rings in my ears constantly. I don't want to be reminded of that night. Keep your thoughts to yourself, I beg of you.'

Anna knew there was no point in speaking to her sister of what else had happened that night, when most of the guests at the banquet had left for their beds. She opened her mouth to say something and then changed her mind. Better not, she thought. She'll bite my head off if I so much as mention it. That was the night when I realized that there was something more going on than the mutual attraction of a man and a woman, and that the Gods had made it their business to guide these mortals. Now, she reflected bitterly, they have seen the outcome of their work. They have destroyed my sister. Anna knew the Gods might be aware of her thoughts but she didn't care. Let them know what I think. They are responsible for everything that's happened.

'Queen Dido,' Aeneas said, turning to her, 'it's going to be hard for me, speaking about some of these things. But I can see that you and the rest of the company want to hear them, so I'll begin at the beginning.'

Everyone in the banqueting hall fell silent as he spoke and leaned forward in their seats. Some filled their goblets with wine from the jars set along the tables; others took another handful of dates or a bunch of grapes from the golden platters laden with fruit. Women gathered their robes around them and settled down for a good story and the men bent their heads to catch Aeneas' words. At first Anna was too preoccupied to listen to him. She went over the whole evening in her head, checking that everything had gone according to her plans.

The feast had been prepared in something of a hurry, but still, as each dish was brought in, the company paused to admire it: first the fish, their silvery, scaly skin stuck with wild herbs, then the roasted fowl – and Anna congratulated both herself and the kitchen staff on the centrepiece of a beautiful peacock, reassembled in the full glory of its plumage. Then four wild boars turned on the spit till their skin glistened brown and crispy, lying on beds of green leaves with their mouths open, as though even in death they were grinning at those who were about to tear into their flesh. Heaped platters of honeyed cakes and fruits came after the meats, and even Aeneas, caught up in his story, stopped in mid-sentence and spent some time picking the translucent ruby seeds from the skin of a pomegranate with the point of a small knife. Yes, Anna thought. This is the best Carthage has to offer and no one can say we have failed in our hospitality. It was only when she was sure that things had been as near to perfect as possible that she relaxed and began to listen to their guest's tales of the great war in Troy.

When Aeneas finished speaking, no one moved for a long time. Those sitting at the long table were silent, thinking of the city far away, making pictures in their heads of Troy set aflame and destroyed while the night was at its darkest; weeping into their sleeves at the thought of the Trojans either killed or imprisoned and the Greeks triumphant. Then, slowly, talk began to flow again. Anna, sitting opposite Aeneas and her sister, was uncharacteristically silent and listened to their conversation.

'Your stories have enthralled everyone, Aeneas. I'm proud to welcome you to Carthage. Take more wine. Your throat must be parched.'

'Thank you, Queen Dido. I'm grateful for your kind words. I've not seen such fine rooms for many years. This palace is grander even than King Priam's.' The intricate gold leaf painted on every beam; the silver-embroidered hangings on the walls; the gold-plated dishes on which the food had been served: you couldn't be in the palace more than a moment without realizing that this queen was a rich and prosperous ruler, well-used to all the luxury that gold could buy.

'My late husband, Sychaeus,' Dido said, 'saw to it that his wealth remained in my hands.'

One by one the guests took their leave and soon the room was nearly empty except for a few privileged courtiers and the sleepy servants, still standing ready to fetch anything the queen might require. Anna was aware that her own eyelids were beginning to feel heavy, and no wonder. She'd not stopped working, overseeing the banquet, since the arrival of Aeneas and his men the day before. I should go to my bed, she thought, and offer prayers that I do not see the fires of Troy in my dreams. The terrible solid bulk of that enormous wooden horse . . . She shivered, and then a cry made her turn to the main door of the banqueting hall.

'Father! Father!' A boy's high voice rose to the high-beamed ceiling. Ascanius, dressed in his nightshirt, ran across the tiled floor. Such a pretty little boy! Anna looked at him, and as usual when she saw a small child, a sharp pain assailed her, making her heart sore for a moment with longing for a baby of her own. Elissa, who was now the boy's nursemaid and whom Anna had left in charge of Ascanius, was hovering nervously near the door. Anna rose to her feet and went to speak with her, while the boy climbed on to his father's lap and clung to his neck.

'Shouldn't he be asleep?' Anna whispered.

'He was. I don't know what happened. He woke up. I was sitting on the stool next to his bed and I think I must have dropped off too, because I'm sure what I saw was a dream.'

'What do you mean? What did you see?'

'Aphrodite – the Goddess of Love. She was floating above the ground . . . Oh, of course I must have been dreaming. She said something to Ascanius. She smelled of roses and her dress . . . It looked . . . well, it didn't look like plain cloth, but like a garment made of mist.'

'Did she speak to you? Say anything?'

Elissa shook her head. 'No, she was whispering to the boy. And then he got up, and she . . . I couldn't see her any longer, though I could smell her perfume. I suppose that proves she was real, but—'

'Don't be a silly girl. Of course she was real. Everybody's real.'

'Maybe it wasn't the Goddess. She didn't speak to me. Perhaps she was a ghost.'

'Nonsense. Whose ghost?'

'The boy's mother.'

Anna had to concede that the child's mother was very likely to return to gaze at her child, even speak to him, after death. She said, 'Well, perhaps, but never mind that. What happened then?'

'He got up and wouldn't let me put him back to bed again. I thought perhaps he was looking for Maron because he's used to being put to bed by him, but he ran out of the room and I followed him here, and now

67

his father will be angry with me, won't he?' Elissa's eyes glittered with unshed tears.

'He seems very happy to see his son, my dear,' Anna said. 'Don't worry any more. Go to your room. I'll attend to the child when he needs to go back to his bed. You'll be rising quite early with him in the morning, I predict.'

'Thank you, madam,' Elissa said, and almost ran out of the room, grateful to hear that she wasn't in trouble.

The flames in the lanterns were guttering. Black shadows moved in the corners of the room and flickered on the walls, and at the table only Dido and Aeneas were left talking. And me, Anna thought. And now Aeneas' son, who had climbed down from his father's lap and run off to explore this new place he found himself in. I'll keep an eye on him, she thought. My sister and the Trojan seem more interested in one another than in the child. Before Ascanius arrived in the room, Anna had wondered whether she ought to go and leave the two of them alone together but had decided she ought to stay. It would be . . . what was the right word? *Unseemly* – yes, unseemly without a doubt – for the Queen of Carthage to show such great favour straight away to someone who, for all his good qualities, was a stranger to them. Her attention was caught by Ascanius, who'd collected date stones from the platters and was playing a complicated game on the benches with some wooden spoons he'd taken from the end of the table.

Then she saw her: the ghost, or Aphrodite, or

whatever she was, hovering near Ascanius and bending down to whisper in the boy's ear. She was just as Elissa had described her: pale, floating garments edged with silver bells that tinkled and chimed as she moved. Anna blinked, stood up and backed away, thinking to call someone – a guard; anyone – and see who this person was, drifting about the palace without announcing her presence, and then she saw that the child was bathed in a blue light and the woman was handing him something – what was it? An arrow? How could that be? Who would do such a thing? Giving a child that age a weapon of any kind! She forgot at once about calling the guard and ran across to where Ascanius was sitting. By the time she'd knelt down beside him, the woman – ghost or goddess or whatever she was – had disappeared. There was a perfume hanging in the air, of roses and almond blossom, but Anna ignored it and said: 'What's that, darling? What have you got in your hand?'

'Nothing,' said the boy, hiding something behind his back.

'Show me now – I saw— Well, never mind, but I do want to see what it is. If I close my eyes, will you put it into my hands?'

Ascanius nodded, as though this would be a good game. Anna dutifully shut her eyes and held out her hands. Something long and rough, like a stick broken off a tree, was placed on her palms and she closed her fingers around it. The child giggled. Anna opened her eyes.

'Why, it's nothing but a silly old stick from the court-yard!' she exclaimed, thinking: I've certainly drunk too much wine. Drifting ladies and bells and shining arrows – it was Elissa's tale that put such things into my mind. 'Who gave it to you? There are no sticks allowed in here, you know. This is the banqueting hall.'

'My mummy. My mummy did.'

Anna put down the stick and hugged the little boy to her, breathing in the fragrance of his hair, feeling his small bones against her body. How fragile he was! How thin! And missing his mother, of course he was. Tears began to fill her eyes and she murmured: 'Come to your bed now, Ascanius. I'll take you.'

He wriggled out of her grasp and ran to the table. 'No!' he cried. 'Don't want bed. Want to stay here.'

Anna got to her feet, but she was too late. The boy had run up to where his father and Dido were sitting. He'd picked up the stick again and was wielding it above his head like a weapon. Anna saw exactly what happened next, and though she went over and over it in the days that followed, she was certain about what she saw, and even today, after all that had happened, she knew she had not been fuddled by wine, or sleepy, or otherwise not herself. She saw this: Ascanius, messing about on his father's lap with his stick, began waving it around in a manner that seemed wild and dangerous to Anna. Aeneas tried to get hold of it, and still Ascanius whirled it above his head, and then Dido said, 'Come to me, Ascanius. Come and sit with me for a while.'

She leaned forward and picked up the boy, and held him against her. Anna saw her sister's arms go round the child and hug him to her bosom. That in itself was strange enough. Dido had never, even when they were young girls, been a cuddler of babies and toddlers. Indeed, she could often barely muster a polite coo if someone was showing off their offspring. Now here she was, seemingly besotted by this boy. There was a faint glow about him, Anna thought, and then: I must be mistaken. How can he be glowing? And the stick – that had become an arrow again, made of some glassy, translucent substance that looked like lightning, solidified into a thin column of radiance with a sharp tip that was piercing her sister just in the place where her necklaces ended, under her left breast.

Anna ran forward. 'Dido! Sister, are you wounded? Hurt?'

'Whatever are you talking about, Anna?' Dido laughed. 'It'd take more than a boy's stick to hurt me. Look . . .' She had grasped the stick (now brown and obviously nothing more than a small branch from some tree) and put it down on the table.

Anna stared at Dido and also at Ascanius. The child was asleep. How could that be? She said: 'Is he well? Just a moment ago he was playing and shouting and waving an imaginary weapon about.'

'That's children for you.' Aeneas stood up and went to take his son from Dido's arms. 'They can fall asleep in the blink of an eye, like candles being snuffed out. It's time we were both in our beds. I'll carry him there. I thank you, Queen Dido, for a memorable feast.'

'We'll speak tomorrow, Aeneas. I'm very happy to be welcoming you to Carthage.'

As father and son left the hall, Anna noticed the stick again, lying on the table. Was it anything like a shining arrow? No, of course not. She picked it up and held it to her bosom. Perhaps it still held a certain magic within it. Aphrodite, she said silently to herself, visit me. Make Iopas love me. Help me to be beautiful in his eyes.

She had thought she might mention what she'd seen to Dido but decided not to. Her sister in any case was far away, leaning back against her cushions, with her eyes closed and a smile on her lips as though she were dreaming of something delightful. Around her, the air seemed to glow with a radiance like starlight.

Just after sunset; a small bedchamber

'You should go now, Anna,' Dido said, and Anna started up from her thoughts, her memories of the night of the feast suddenly interrupted.

'I've been dreaming, but you're right. I need to see that the bed is being properly guarded in the court-yard, but I think you want to get rid of me. Don't pretend.'

'I want to be alone, that's true enough. It's not you, Anna. I feel – I can't say how I feel.'

'I'll come back,' Anna said. 'Don't think you're getting rid of me for the night. And I almost forgot. I've got something for you. I should have given it to you at once. It's a sleeping draught. I had the healer prepare his special mixture. Poppies and honey and something very secret he prefers not to mention. Here, take the phial.'

'I'm not interested in sleeping. Why can't you get that into your head? Take it away. I want nothing to do with sleeping draughts. I've tried the healer's potion before and it made me feel as though I was out of my own body. As though I was walking around in a dream. Then, when I slept, I couldn't wake up for a very long time. I don't want it.'

'I'll put it on the windowsill,' Anna said. 'Just in case.'

Dido said nothing, either about the sleeping draught or anything else. She smiled to show that she was in a more normal state now and could therefore be left on her own for a while.

Elissa

After the evening meal; the maidservants' bedchamber

'What's wrong, Elissa? Tell us. You've not stopped crying for hours.' Nezral, who was thin and fair, with a beaky nose that gave her something of the look of a bird of prey, came to where she was sitting on the edge of her bed and put an arm around her shoulders. Elissa, overcome by this display of kindness, began to cry even more noisily, and soon her nose was running and her eyes, sore from the tears she'd shed earlier in the afternoon, stung even more than before. The lamps were still burning because the girls had been unable to fall asleep with so much going on in the corridors of the palace.

'Take a cloth for your nose,' said Tanith, holding out a square of cotton and sitting down on the other side of Elissa. 'You were so kind to me this morning, when I was crying about Maron. And though I'm still sad, you know that we'll listen if you want to tell us why you're so unhappy.'

'Take no notice of her,' Nezral was quick to interrupt. 'We both know exactly why you're crying. We know you loved him.'

'Who? Who am I supposed to have loved?'

Tanith blushed. 'Lord Aeneas,' she said. 'We've known from the beginning that you loved him.'

'How? I said nothing. Not one word.' Elissa was indignant.

'You didn't need to,' Nezral said. 'We could hear the way your voice changed when you spoke his name. You were always blushing. And quick to come to his defence if anyone said a single word against him.'

'I was loyal to him, that's all,' Elissa said. 'I was his son's nursemaid. Oh, how I'll miss that boy!' The tears began to flow again and she wiped her face with the damp cotton rag in her hands. Suddenly she jumped up from the bed. 'Oh, I have to go – I'm sick. I must find . . .' She fled from the room, running along the corridor to the privy. Once she was there, she began to vomit. Nezral and Tanith had followed her, and when the worst of the spasms were over, the two of them ran to Elissa's side and led her gently to the jugs of water which stood in the bathing area. Nezral took a scoop of water and held it out to her friend.

'Drink, Elissa. You're ill. Is it any wonder, with the amount of crying you've been doing? Come, come back to our chamber. Lie down. Tanith, go and find the healer and see if he'll come and see to Elissa.'

'No, no, please,' Elissa said. 'I don't want to see the healer. I'll be all right in a moment. I must be tired, as you say. And unhappy. I've been vomiting on and off for a few days. Perhaps it's something in the food. It'll pass, whatever's caused it.'

Once the girls were back in their chamber, Tanith and Nezral helped Elissa to undress and she lay under the coverlet on her bed, shivering and wanting nothing more than to sleep and sleep. Tanith sat beside her on a stool and held her hand.

'Elissa,' she whispered, 'how long have you been ill? Why have you said nothing?'

'Not very long. A few days, that's all. I thought it would pass, but it seems to be worse than it was . . .' Her voice faded away.

'You know, don't you,' Nezral said, from where she was sitting on her own bed, 'what this might mean?'

'What? What are you talking about?' Elissa made as if to sit up and sank back weakly on to her pillows, nearly overwhelmed with nausea.

'Don't be angry,' Tanith said, 'but vomiting at unexpected times can mean that you are pregnant.'

Elissa sat up then and shouted, 'No! No, I can't be. How can I be?'

Both Nezral and Tanith giggled. 'You know how you can be, Elissa! Don't be stupid. You have to lie with a man. Have you done that? Who is it? How can it be that you have a sweetheart and haven't told us? What about Iopas? He's always gazing after you and visiting the sewing room for one reason or another when you're in there. And I saw you talking together on the bench earlier this afternoon.

He's got a crush on you, I'm quite sure of it.'

'He was just being polite. And whatever he might feel, I haven't got a crush on him. I like him well enough, but the very idea of . . . well, of what you're suggesting. I'd never do that with him.' Elissa suddenly covered her face with her hands and cried. 'But what shall I do now? How can it be true? I can't—'

'Calm yourself!' Nezral tried to sound firm and soothing at the same time. 'We all know how it can be true. Have you been with a man? Answer truthfully now. Is it possible at least?'

Elissa nodded and began to cry again. 'Yes – but only once. I didn't think if you did it just once . . . I didn't realize. I thought . . . It was just one night.'

'Don't get too upset yet. It's not the only sign. When was the last time you bled?'

'I don't remember. Some moons ago, I think.'

A silence fell in the room. No one knew what to say. At last Elissa spoke, but so quietly that her companions had to lean forward to hear what she was saying. 'It's my doing. I'm shouting and weeping now, but I longed for this. I didn't dare to hope, after only one night. I prayed for a child. I thought that if he knew I was having a baby, that would hold him to me, keep him at my side. I didn't know. The night we were together I thought he loved me, but he didn't. Not really. He has – he had – eyes for no one but the queen. I'm a fool. And now I've been punished.'

'Are you speaking of Lord Aeneas?' Nezral asked. She and Tanith sat with their mouths gaping open in astonishment. 'How did it happen? When? We knew you were besotted with him, but we never thought for a moment that he was interested in you. All his attention has been on the queen. You said so yourself. Why didn't you tell us?'

'I was frightened,' Elissa answered. 'I didn't want anyone to know, but especially not Dido. She must never find out about this. Never ever. Do you both promise? If she does, she'll send me back to my parents' house. And if she doesn't discover that Aeneas is the father, she might look for a husband for me, and I can't love anyone but Aeneas. What am I going to do?'

'You'll have to get rid of the baby.' Nezral spoke impassively and Elissa burst into tears once more.

'How can you even say such a thing? It makes me ill to think of it. I've seen what happens when you go to those crones whose business it is to perform abortions. Sometimes they don't get rid of the child, but take you away – imprison you and wait for the birth and then help themselves to your son or daughter and you never see your baby again. I've heard such horrible stories. I'm not going to them. I couldn't.'

'If you like, I can find out if there's a plant extract or potion you could take that would lead to you bleeding again,' said Nezral. 'Naturally, I mean. It's true – imagining the ways those old women rid the body of a baby is too dreadful to think about. But my aunt is a midwife, and she'd know. If I told her what had happened to you, I'm sure she'd help us.'

'No,' Elissa said. 'No, I must have this baby. I want it.

I want to love it for as long as it lives, because it will remind me of him. Of Aeneas.'

'But what'll you say when it becomes impossible to hide your condition? When the baby is born?' Nezral had begun, Elissa noticed, to sound irritated. Why was that? Could it be envy? Or was she simply angry at the stupidity of a friend? She sounded crosser and crosser the longer she spoke. 'You have to think of your future, Elissa. Who's going to want to marry you with another man's bastard in the house? Not even Iopas would be as forgiving as that. What will you tell Dido when she asks you who the father is? You have to think about these matters, however unpleasant it might be.'

'Stop nagging me, Nezral. I know what you're saying is true, but I'm prepared for this. I don't care if I never marry. I'll look after my baby by myself. And I'll lie to Dido. I'll invent a lover. What does she know about who I see and speak to when I'm not in the palace? Why should she care? Don't worry about me. Or my baby.'

'If anyone should ask you why you're so sad,' Tanith said, and Elissa was relieved that her tone was gentler and more soothing than Nezral's, 'tell them you're weeping for little Ascanius. They'll understand that. They'll sympathize. *What a tender-hearted girl that Elissa is*, they'll say. *Mourning the boy she's had the care of for so long*. Most people will accept that, and you'll be safe for a short while at least.'

Elissa closed her eyes. Tanith went on, 'That's right. You should sleep. You'll feel better tomorrow.'

Elissa knew that sleep would be a long time coming to her tonight, if it came at all. She lay quietly as her friends prepared for bed, and found the sadness she'd felt at the harbour, knowing she would never again see Aeneas, returning to overwhelm her, even though she'd tried as hard as she could to be calmer. She couldn't help regretting . . . well, regretting a great many things when she thought about it. But regret wouldn't help her either. I'm too young to go into mourning for ever, she told herself. I couldn't help what I did, and I don't regret loving Aeneas. He would be gone at daybreak, and what use was weeping? She had to do everything in her power to look after herself, because Dido was the only person in the world who would care for her, but that would end in an eyeblink if the queen found out who the father of her baby was. If that happened, she would be banished, sent into exile, even (and this was the worst fate that she could imagine) sent home to her father's house. She remembered her miserable home in the hills above the city and her family: a cruel father who'd sell his daughter (because she was a daughter and not a son) for the price of a drink or marry her to a brute, and a mother who was too cowed and beaten by her husband's drunken fists to stop him doing it. And too many brothers and sisters to share what was there to be shared.

I won't allow such things to happen to my child, Elissa thought. I'll be a good mother to this baby, even if others think I'm nothing and nobody. I'll be its mother. The most important person in the child's world. Her pregnancy would be visible quite soon. What she had told her friends wasn't quite true. She'd suspected for a few days that a baby might be growing in her body. She had seen enough women (starting with her own mother) feeling ill, tired and listless in the early part of their pregnancies. Even that night, on the one occasion when she had lain down with Aeneas (and she tried as hard as she could not to think of it because it made her want to cry even more), the notion that she might have a baby as a consequence had come into her mind. Since then, she'd lain in her bed each night and stared at the ceiling, praying to the Gods to look on her with favour and allow her to be the mother of Aeneas' child. The old women always said: *Be careful what you ask the Gods to give you*, and they were right. Her prayers had been answered, and what good was that? She'd asked for the wrong thing. She should have implored them to keep him here in Carthage. It was too late now and she wished that she'd made more of a fuss earlier, when she was down at the harbour. She ought to have called out: *I'm going to be the mother of his child.* But his soldiers would have laughed at her. Sent her packing. I don't look as if I could be anyone's mother, she reflected. I'm too thin and small and dark and girlish. Her breasts, which were not enormous, would grow bigger to feed this baby, and part of her was longing for that. She envied some of the other young women who worked with her in the sewing room who, even though they were the same age as herself, looked much older and had to deal constantly with young men pinching their bottoms as they went about the city and whistling after them and making lewd remarks.

She wished that her friends hadn't discovered the truth about her and Aeneas, even though she was fairly sure they would keep her secret – at least for a while. But what if they didn't? What if Dido found something out from them? She would have to ensure their silence in whatever ways she could think of. It was going to be a long night, and Elissa closed her eyes. She would go back, she resolved, to remembering the morning Dido had introduced her to the man she would grow to love.

'Elissa! Queen Dido has sent for you. You're to go at once to the south terrace, please.' Anna smiled and beckoned Elissa with her finger. Tanith had just come into the sewing room and whispered in Anna's ear, and Elissa stood up, folded her work neatly and prepared to leave the room. I wish I didn't have to go, she thought. The sewing room was on the shady side of the palace when the sun was at its height and the thick walls meant that you could stay cool there even when the weather was stiflingly hot. And you could sit down while you were working, and talk to your companions in a soft voice, and sometimes Anna would bring in sweets and small cakes as a treat for her young ladies, as she liked to call the women and girls who sat around the long tables. But if the queen wanted to see her, then of course she had to drop everything she was doing and get to wherever she had to be as quickly as she could. By the time she reached the south terrace Elissa was quite out of breath.

'You've been running, child,' Dido said, smiling at her. 'Sit down here for a moment and catch your breath.'

Elissa sat down and looked around her. The south terrace was beautiful. Greenery had been trained to cover wide arches and the stone seats had been placed in the shade. They were high above the city here, and you could look down and see all the new dwellings that Dido had ordered to be built around the harbour. The houses clustered together and the streets were lined with palm trees, planted to make shade for those who lived there. A breeze was blowing off the ocean, making the heat more bearable. Sitting next to Dido was Ascanius' father, the Trojan prince, Aeneas. This was the second time she'd seen him. He'd come to kiss his son goodnight the previous evening, but he hadn't stayed very long, and in any case Elissa had been occupied with going through the little boy's clothes and making a note of what he needed, and she hadn't paid any particular attention to this devoted father. She looked at him now and was embarrassed to meet his eyes. He was smiling at her and it was impossible for her not to smile back.

'It was kind of you to sit with my son while he slept last night,' said Aeneas, and Elissa found herself wishing he would go on speaking. He had a voice sweeter than music played on instruments and she felt at that moment that she would happily listen to him for ever.

'I was glad to help,' she said. 'He's such a sweet baby.'

'He won't like you calling him that. He's nearly four years old and thinks that's grown up. If you asked him, he'd tell you he was a big boy.'

'Of course,' Elissa said. 'No one likes to be called a baby. I'll be more careful when I speak to him.'

'I hope,' Dido said, 'that you will agree to what I'm going to suggest to you. I know my sister values your skill in the sewing room, and of course you often help my own handmaidens with my clothes and jewels, but I think it would put Lord Aeneas' mind at rest if he knew that you would be Ascanius' permanent nursemaid. I hope very much that you will enjoy the work. Tell me what you think, Elissa. He's been in the care of Maron but I feel a girl would be more . . . well, more suitable.'

'Oh, yes, my lady,' said Elissa. 'It would be an honour. Ascanius is a sweet boy and I think he likes me. And Maron . . . he's been very good with him, of course, but I'll enjoy looking after him. I know I will.'

Almost as though he'd been waiting for this to be arranged, Ascanius burst out from behind an enormous terracotta jar overflowing with flowers. Maron, who'd been so funny last night, making her and Tanith laugh with his antics as they were getting Ascanius ready for bed, was just behind the boy and waved a hand at Elissa to show he recognized her.

'I'm hiding,' Ascanius shouted. 'No one came to find me. I'll hide again. Elissa, *you* come and find me. Count to ten and then come.'

Elissa stood up and started counting at once: 'One . . . two . . . three . . .'

'I'm ready.' Ascanius had run back behind the jar. 'Come and find me.'

'Where can Ascanius be?' Elissa said, pretending she had no idea. As she crept around the terrace, looking in all the wrong places, she was suddenly reminded of the games she'd never been able to play with her little brothers and sisters, and tears came into her eyes. Would she ever see any of them again? Did they miss her? Speak of her? Wonder what had happened to her? Did her mother cry into her pillow at night, grieving for her eldest daughter? She shook her head to clear it of such thoughts and said loudly: 'What's happened to Ascanius? I can't find him anywhere—'

'I'm here!' shouted Ascanius, emerging from his hiding place.

'So you are,' Elissa said. The boy came running up to her and flung his arms around her knees. She bent down to hug him, stroking his brown curls, feeling his body against her legs. It was fragile and small and yet it held within it the promise of a man's strength, his father's vigour. Elissa shivered. She looked at Aeneas and he was smiling straight at her.

'He's very fond of you,' he said. 'That's good. I want him to be happy more than I want anything in this world.'

'I'll look after him,' Elissa said, watching the little boy as he ran off again. 'He's the same age as one of my own brothers. You don't have to worry about him.

We'll stay here till it's time for his supper. Then I'll bathe him and put him to bed.'

'And I'll come and kiss him goodnight. Thank you, Elissa.'

Elissa blushed and found herself longing for that hour. Ascanius would be in bed, and Aeneas would come to his room and she'd be there, and then . . . She couldn't imagine what would happen then. She would be in Aeneas' presence again, that was the main thing. How silly she was! Looking forward to the next time she might see him when he was still here, in front of her, and even speaking to her. I'm mad, she told herself. I'm being ridiculous.

'Thank you, Elissa,' said Dido. She stood up and turned to Aeneas, offering him her hand. He sprang up at once and they went off together. The queen kept her eyes firmly on the path in front of them, but Aeneas turned back and waved. At his son – because there was Ascanius, waving back – but also at me, Elissa thought as she lifted her arm. He may have been waving at the boy, but the smile was for me. How do you know that? she asked herself. How do you know it was for you? I just do, Elissa answered her own question. I could tell.

She was going over the moment in her mind when Maron came up to her and said, 'Are you happy to be alone with Ascanius for a while? Or would you like me to stay for a bit?'

'Could you tell me a little about him? The kinds of things you do with him. I told Lord Aeneas that I had a brother of his age, but I've never looked after a child all by myself. It's a bit . . . well, a bit alarming.'

Maron sat down on a stone bench and smiled. 'You'll do very well, I think. I'll talk to him . . . Here, Ascanius. Come over here.'

The little boy looked up from the sand in which he was making marks with a pointed stick. Elissa wondered for a moment if it was safe for such a small child to have something that looked as though it could turn into a weapon at any moment, but before she could say anything Ascanius had thrown the stick away and come over to where Maron was sitting.

'What?' he said, and jumped on to Maron's knee.

'You've met Elissa,' Maron said. 'But I want you to say: *Hello, Elissa, I'm going to be the best boy in the world for you.* Go on, say it!'

Ascanius giggled and began to pull Maron's red hair. 'Stop that, you little monkey!' said Maron, but you could tell he wasn't angry. He was grinning and pulled playfully on Ascanius' hair. 'I can pull harder than you can, so you'd better just *stop*!'

Elissa wondered whether she ought to tell Maron to be serious, to be more grown up, but then decided not to.

'I'm as much of a kid as he is – that's what you're thinking, isn't it?'

'No, not really,' Elissa said.

'I can see that you're not used to telling fibs. You're blushing . . . It's all right. I *am* a bit of a kid, and I don't care who knows it. We get on fine, don't we, Ascanius?

87

As long as you do what I say. And you must do *exactly* what Elissa says from now on. She's going to be looking after you.'

Ascanius ran over to Elissa and smiled up at her. 'Good!' he shouted. 'Elissa won't pull my hair. She's nicer than you are. You're horrible.'

'I'm much more horrible than you think,' Maron said, laughing. 'I'm a monster.' He stood up and formed his hands into claws and began to chase Ascanius around the garden. The two of them ran about with their faces twisted and their arms raised above their heads, shrieking loudly.

'Stop! Both of you. Stop at once.' Elissa was surprised how loudly she could shout when she had to.

Maron caught Ascanius and swung him up on to his shoulders. He came over to where Elissa was standing and lifted him down to the ground.

'Enough fooling around, right, Ascanius? We're going to be as good and quiet as little lambs from now on.'

'Not a lamb!' Ascanius said. 'A monster!'

'Not any longer,' Maron said firmly. 'Monster time's over for now. Another day we'll play monsters again.'

He turned to Elissa and said, 'Will you do something for me, Elissa?'

'Of course I will. I'm very grateful for your help with Ascanius.'

'It's about Tanith . . . is that her name? The curly-haired dark girl?'

'Yes, Tanith . . . What about her?' Elissa smiled and

added: 'As though I can't guess. You want me to put in a good word for you, is that it?'

Maron ran his fingers through his hair, pushing it off his forehead. He said, 'Yes, that'd be great. If you don't mind.'

'Of course not. And now you're the one who's blushing.'

'Naah . . .' said Maron. 'Not really. It's a hot day. I've been in the sun too long. I burn very easily. It's having red hair, you know. But thanks. For your help, I mean. Have fun with Ascanius.'

He ran ahead of her and winked as he disappeared into the shade of the colonnades.

Elissa smiled. *Have fun.* Maron was good at fun. He went through life enjoying everything. Some God must have smiled on him when he was born.

The early part of the night; the maidservants' bedchamber

That was the first day, she reflected, lying on her back on the bed. Tanith and Nezral were breathing deeply but Elissa gazed into the darkness, still unable to fall asleep. I did a good thing for Tanith. I told her what Maron said and she was so happy about it. Or maybe it wasn't a good thing at all, because now he's gone and she's sad. But she wouldn't have wanted *not* to love Maron. I'm sure of that. And I was right about Aeneas too, she thought. He *had* been smiling at me, and what I understood in that look was there. It was. It truly was.

Iopas

Iopas stood at the window of his bedchamber, looking down at the city and, beyond that, the harbour. The moonlight fell on a landscape of roofs, which during the day made a complicated pattern of russet brown and gold and white and black, with the gardens of the larger houses showing like splashes of green. Now, clouds lay in wispy strands along the horizon and he could see the whole of Carthage, with its fine houses and temples and shops and workshops and markets spread out around the bay, leeched of their colour and seeming to be a uniform silvery grey. Points of light, like tiny yellow flowers, shone from the windows. Down on the sea, Aeneas' ships waited for the dawn tide. Small figures, probably guards, stood at the entrance to the harbour. The Trojan was leaving. Well, Iopas thought, I for one was expecting it. There isn't much I don't know of what goes on in this place.

Because of his quietness, the natural shyness that

made it difficult for him to speak much in public unless he was performing, he had managed to learn a great deal. If he came into a room, for the most part the people in it didn't stop talking on his account. You could discover a great many secrets like that, and you could also contrive to spend time in places which you'd normally steer clear of. He didn't mind being the way he was except when it came to Elissa. Iopas knew that he'd missed an opportunity earlier, when they'd been sitting together on the bench in the corridor. Perhaps he should have been braver and said something about his feelings. For a long time he'd been able to see that she was besotted with Aeneas, but no one else seemed to realize so he said nothing. Even now that he was gone, she wasn't ready to speak about it. He sighed.

When Elissa first came to the palace, he'd been struck by her beauty, and the fact that she'd run away from home made him feel protective. She was no more than a pretty child then, but over the years she'd spent as a servant in the palace, she'd become a young woman and Iopas had noted the changes carefully. As she grew, so did his affection for her. Now, he told himself, it would be true to say I love her. He never spoke either to Elissa or to anyone else about his feelings but she was always quite friendly. I *was* jealous of her crush on the Trojan, he thought, but no one would have known just by looking at me. He sighed. For a long time, whenever he found himself dwelling on Elissa's admiration for Aeneas, he'd had to keep himself carefully under control. The last thing he wanted was anyone feeling sorry for him, or thinking that Elissa actually preferred someone else. Anyway it was completely ridiculous for a mere servant to nurse a passion for someone so far above her in status. Madness. Aeneas was not only a prince, but the man who shared the queen's bed, although it was true that lately the two of them had been more distant and were even heard to quarrel on occasion. Elissa hadn't seemed to mind talking to him today, even though she was obviously feeling bad. It could be, he told himself, that with Aeneas gone, I might be in with a chance.

Burying himself in his work had helped with his frustration. When he was performing at a feast, or at a smaller gathering, he knew he pleased those who heard him; they would never have guessed at the feelings he was suppressing. His official duties as court poet and singer meant that he had to be on the alert for everything. There were old men in the palace who'd tut-tutted when he was first appointed, but Anna had said: *Who better than a boy of eighteen to write of battles and love and glory?* And the queen had agreed with her in the end. He'd done his best for Dido, honoured and pleased to have been chosen from among those who came to the palace to be examined and looked at and tested. In order to write the songs, Iopas had to know the truth about a great many things, including the feelings of the queen. He felt privileged, almost like a son to her, and enjoyed expressing some of her emotions in his poems. Here was one (he picked the parchment up from his table) which he'd written in honour of the queen and her sister, Anna.

Two sweet birds in one small nest,
two fair flowers on one green stem,
fruits from the same tree: honoured, blessed.
Dido and Anna: praise to them!

The queen often took him into her confidence. But Anna (he smiled at the thought and congratulated himself on putting it so wittily, even if he didn't have an audience to appreciate the wordplay) would far rather have taken him into her bed than her confidence, and did not think of him as a nephew. He'd had to be very diplomatic keeping out of her clutches. She was pleasant enough, and her favour meant that all sorts of perks came to him, one way and another, but he'd resisted her attempts to woo him. He'd invented a girlfriend in the city to whom he'd promised his love and devotion, because you couldn't just come out with it: *I'm sorry, madam, I don't fancy you.* No, the treats and privileges would have dried up for sure if he'd confessed to that, so he kept up the appearance – reasonably successfully, he thought – of someone who would, but for his feelings towards another, have liked nothing better than to make love to the queen's sister.

This lie, which had sprung up all at once when he was defending himself from Anna, had now caught him in a kind of trap. That would be another reason for keeping his feelings for Elissa quiet, he realized. Because of the rapid circulation of gossip in the palace, Anna would soon find out and wonder what had happened to his previous lover and so it would go. For all I know, he thought, Elissa already knows about my 'fiancée' down in the town. Maybe that's one reason why she's a little distant. He sighed. Telling lies led to so many complications. Perhaps now that Aeneas was leaving them, things could be different.

Before finding Elissa on the bench, Iopas had walked around the palace, wondering at the movement and disruption. Anna had closeted herself with Dido for a long time, but Iopas had seen her leaving and hurrying through the palace towards the sewing room. Soldiers had stomped through the corridors moving things and there was now a gigantic bed in the middle of the courtyard, flanked by flowerpots and shaded by tall palm trees. Maids and menservants had spent almost the entire day bringing clothes and weapons and bed linen and coverlets and cushions and piling them on to the bed. A boy whom Iopas recognized as one of the kitchen lads who turned the spits and carried the heavy bags of vegetables from the market – they called him Cubby, and with good reason – sat on the bench beside the bed, not doing much of anything as far as Iopas could see. He wasn't really capable of challenging anyone who had theft in mind, and was in any case unarmed. As soon as he saw him sitting there staring into space, like a pudding on a dish, Iopas decided he no longer felt like exploring the piles of belongings heaped on the bed. He would have had to speak to the boy and didn't fancy that. Perhaps Cubby had that effect on everyone, and that was why he'd been left there. Not a bad plan when you looked at it that way.

Now there was silence everywhere. Iopas felt it was safe to leave his room and walk about a little. He wasn't sure whether there was anything of interest going on, but if there was, he wanted to be around to see it. Some lines came into his mind and he spoke them to himself as he crept through the darkened corridors:

> *Take me with you, over the sea.*
> *Let me sail on the ship that's leaving.*
> *How can I bear to stay on the shore*
> *and spend the rest of my days in grieving?*

He'd written them a long time ago, but they seemed particularly apt in the present circumstances. Dido must be thinking just such thoughts.

Iopas tiptoed past the courtyard and glanced at the bed: Cubby was nowhere to be seen. That surely wasn't right. Someone was sitting on the bench nearest the bed and it wasn't him. Who could it be? What had they done with Cubby? He approached the figure without fear because he could tell that it was a woman. She'd covered her head with some kind of scarf, but how had she persuaded the fat boy to disappear? A movement over by the colonnade made Iopas turn and he caught sight of the kitchen lad, peering round one of

the columns. There wasn't much light in the courtyard, but even at this distance you could see the kid
looked a bit uncomfortable. He decided to go over
and find out what was going on. If it involved conversation with Cubby, that was too bad. He found himself
whispering as he spoke.

'What are you doing here? Aren't you meant to be
guarding the bed?'

'Yes, but the queen told me—'

'The queen? The queen is fast asleep by now, I'd
have thought. What're you talking about?'

Cubby nodded his head towards the figure of the
woman in the courtyard. 'No, she's not asleep. That's
her on my bench. She told me to go away. I came over
here. I didn't want to go away because the master of
the guard put me in charge.'

Iopas heard the pride in the boy's voice. 'Quite
right. You stay where you are. That seems best. Till she
goes to bed. Are you quite sure it's the queen?'

Cubby nodded. 'Yes. It is. But she didn't look like
she normally looks. She looked sad. And her hair was
a real mess.'

'I'll go and speak with her.'

'She said she wanted to be alone.'

'The queen and I,' Iopas said, unable to resist boast-
ing, 'have a very special relationship.'

Cubby nodded. Iopas wondered if he knew the word
relationship and concluded that he probably didn't. He
stepped out into the courtyard. In the dark, the palm
trees, planted especially to create shade when the sun

was at its highest, were like a forest composed of shadows and the shadows of shadows. I must remember that, he told himself. *Shadows and the shadows of shadows* – it would do for a poem.

'Madam,' he said quietly as he came up behind the queen, 'is it you? Can I do something for you? Help you?'

'Iopas!' Dido turned round, and in the dim light of the stars and a quarter moon he could see that she was smiling at him. 'Am I in need of help? Oh, you cannot imagine how much help I need! All the help in the world.'

'Can I fetch you some wine or food? Call your sister? Your attendants?'

'No, Iopas, I thank you. But sit here for a while and talk to me. There are some things I want to discuss with you. I meant to send for you, but I've been . . . indisposed. Sit there, on that bench, so that I can see you.'

'Madam,' Iopas said, 'you sound distracted. Not yourself. Are you certain you don't want me to call someone?'

'Stop it!' Dido raised her voice. 'Since this morning I've had nothing but people creeping and crawling about and wanting to do something for me and think-ing they're helping me when everything they do irritates me beyond all reason. Just sit there and listen. It's true I'm not myself. I was someone till today and now I have to turn myself into . . . I don't know what I have to become. It's painful. I don't know if I can live

97

like this. In this pain. I looked down at my city earlier this afternoon. At the buildings and the houses and the temples and gardens, and I cared as little about it as if it were a collection of coloured bricks put together by an infant, which I could kick over with my foot. That's how important Carthage is to me now. Meaningless. Nothing means anything now. Not food, nor air, nor water, nor power, nor riches, nor the future. The only thing I want is my memories of him. I want him and he's gone, and there's nothing under the blue dome of the sky that's worth a dried fig. I came here thinking: If I sit by the bed, I'll be calmer. It will remind me of better days. But everything I look at is like a knife entering my heart. Everything you see on the bed is something that belonged to Aeneas and I can't bear to look at what's there.'

Iopas was on the point of saying: *Then why come here and torture yourself? Why not keep away?* But he understood that that would infuriate Dido.

'*Love,*' he ventured (quoting one of his own lines of poetry and hoping that the queen wouldn't recognize it – he'd sung the song at a feast a few moons ago), '*fills us with madness, fills us with—*' He stopped, realizing that the next word was *joy.* The queen was the very opposite of joyful and it would be tactless to remind her of happier times when she was in this state. He altered it just in time and said instead: '*grief.*'

'Yes,' Dido answered. 'Grief. That's it exactly. As though the object of your love had died. I know all about grief, Iopas. My first husband, my beloved

Sychaeus – he died. Did you know that? He was butchered by my brother. Can you imagine anything so terrible? My love, lying on the floor of our bed-chamber with blood bubbling out of his throat, his eyes like the eyes of a dead fish on a marble slab. I couldn't stay. I couldn't touch him – the man whose every word used to fill me with happiness, the taste of whose lips had been a kind of divine nourishment for me. I ran away. I woke my sister and my servants and we fled like robbers. Till I came to Carthage I didn't know a moment's peace, and even here, though there were many who helped me and were kind to us, though I was occupied with the building of the city, my heart . . .'

Dido made a fist of her hand and struck herself below her left breast, over and over again, till Iopas wondered whether he ought to stop her. Take hold of her arms and prevent her from hurting herself. Surely she would be bruised from such blows? He started up from the stone bench, and the queen smiled suddenly.

'I can see you're worried, Iopas. You think I might harm myself in my sorrow. Well, I might, and I wouldn't care if I did, and neither should you. But you're a gallant soul. I knew that when I chose you to be the court singer. I was right to do so. I'm very satisfied with all your work. All the songs . . .'

'I hope I may write many more for you, madam,' Iopas said.

'I'll come to that.' Dido smiled at him. 'But I want to

know: those first few days after Aeneas arrived on our shores – how well do you remember them?'

'As if they'd just happened.'

'Tell me. Tell me your memories.'

Iopas took a deep breath. Was there anything he should avoid saying? He hadn't been entirely honest with the queen. It was true: he *could* summon up a fair amount from those days (which, after all, were only two summers ago), but there was sure to be much that he'd forgotten, and maybe those were exactly the things the queen wanted to revisit. Well, hesitating wasn't going to help him. He had to say something.

'The whole palace was like a busy market, that's what I remember. So many people bringing things to the kitchen. Suddenly we seemed to need a great deal more food.'

'Thirty people. That's not a couple of unexpected guests, is it? After the first few nights we found quarters for most of the men with families in the city, who were happy to have them. I paid, of course, for their food and board. It's amazing how much you can achieve with gold. But Aeneas . . .'

'You gave orders that he was to be put in the main guest bedchamber. Your sister brought in extra seam-stresses to embroider the linens and window drapes. I think she worked on the more delicate pieces herself.'

Iopas didn't want to dwell too long on the sewing room. In those days Anna had been in the habit of summoning him there just as the sun was setting, saying that her work would be much easier if he sang to her as she sewed. That was a pretext. Iopas knew her real reason for wanting to get him on his own, and avoiding being caught by her in an embrace took a great deal of manoeuvring. Once, he'd not been quite quick enough and found that Anna had placed herself between him and the door as he was on his way out, and she'd actually put her arms around him and pressed herself against him, and her lips were on his before he knew it, and what was he meant to do? He was only human, and she was pleasant and he liked her and her mouth tasted good and he responded for a moment and allowed himself to hug her back and kiss her rather more enthusiastically than he ought to have done. 'Oh, Iopas,' she'd breathed. 'I knew it. I knew you had a fondness for me. I can feel that you do—'

'No, madam . . .' He'd been quick to spring back and dodge round her body, and go and stand with his hand on the door, ready to escape. 'I can't – I mustn't. Please don't tempt me. My future father-in-law will hear of it and then I don't know what might happen. I hate saying this to you, madam, but we mustn't – truly. I'm so sorry. You're right, I *do* have a fondness for you, but I must forget that and put it aside and not endanger my true love.'

To her credit, Anna had behaved very well. She was kind, it occurred to Iopas, and he'd been grateful to her. But whenever she could, she still found ways to be alone with him. She came to the door of his bed-chamber from time to time, and he had to go and stand on the threshold – otherwise, he was sure, she'd have invited herself in and sat on his bed and then contrived to kiss him, and who knows where that would have led? He had to be on his guard all the time. It would not do to offend the queen's sister in case she complained to Dido about him, and then he would find himself thrown out of the palace. Dido would send him packing with no thought or regret for any work he'd done. He sighed and tried to remember what those first few days had been like.

'Take your time,' Dido said. 'There's no rush.'

Iopas had never known the palace to be so full of people. Everywhere you went, you tripped over one of the new guests – men who'd come ashore with Aeneas and who in another life had been Trojan soldiers. Their manners were not exactly delicate and they were very noisy and boisterous, and some of them rampaged through the corridors making such a racket that the master of the guard had been forced to turn them out into the gardens for most of the day. The only person who'd bothered to speak to him was Maron, who was not much more than a boy but seemed a pleasant fellow. He'd come into Iopas' room on his first day at the palace and said, just as though he were a long-lost friend: 'Hello! I know who you are – the poet who sang to us last night. Iopas, right?'

'Right,' said Iopas, echoing the word, though it wasn't the kind of thing he said naturally.

'Maron, that's me. I've been given a room just down there' – he pointed towards the end of the corridor –

'but I thought I'd do a bit of exploring. Don't you get bored, writing poems all day long?'

He'd come into the room and somehow settled himself on Iopas' only chair, even though he hadn't been invited to sit down. Iopas, still standing, said, 'No, I don't. There are so many things that ask to be written about.'

'Like . . . ?' Maron smiled up at him. 'Read me one of your poems. I can't read myself, but I like a nice song. You don't have to sing if you don't feel like it. But I'd like to hear a few verses.'

'Oh!' That was one thing Iopas couldn't resist: someone asking to hear his words. He picked up a piece of parchment and said, 'Well, I won't sing this one – my lyre is over there but one of the strings needs changing. This is about great men being brought low.' He cleared his throat and began to speak:

> '*Even the straightest and the tallest tree*
> *which stands above the rest and lets its leaves*
> *provide cool shadows on the hottest day –*
> *why, even that tree can be cut and felled*
> *by fatal strokes from one man's silver axe.*'

'That's not bad,' said Maron, looking as though he really meant it. 'The tree's supposed to be like the man, is that it? You're saying that however big a hero someone is, there's someone else even bigger and fiercer who can cut him down to size.'

'Exactly!' said Iopas. The boy may not have been able to read, but he was clearly very intelligent.

'Well, it's good to meet you. I've got to go and find Ascanius now, or he'll be getting into some kind of mischief.' Maron stood up and went over to where Iopas' lyre was lying on the table. He ran his fingers over the untuned strings and Iopas winced at the sound. 'Sorry,' said Maron. 'Couldn't resist!'

He was gone before Iopas could object.

After that first day Dido and the Trojan fell into the habit of going on long walks through the city and Iopas thought that she did this to show off for his benefit. Whenever he could, he accompanied them as part of the train of courtiers and guards who followed the queen wherever she went. In the streets of Carthage, as she passed, everyone bowed almost to the ground, and she smiled at them and made a sign with her hand for them to stand upright, and then they'd wave and smile and she would bow her head, and the servants who walked behind her and Aeneas carrying sunshades had to keep well out of the way so that everyone got a good view. Every so often she and Aeneas would stop and speak to a shopkeeper, or a builder on one of the many new sites around the city where yet another splendid building was rising out of the earth. Iopas could see, from the way the queen leaned towards Aeneas, that she was in love with him. He'd had enough experience of seeing common people in the throes of passion and it was a little disappointing to realize that royal personages were no different. Dido tossed her head flirtatiously, looked up at the Trojan through her eyelashes and licked her lips to moisten them. Iopas wasn't close enough to over-hear any words, but laughter carried to him on the air, and even though the heat was often intense, when they stopped to admire anything, they stood very close to one another. Sometimes Aeneas gave Dido his hand as they moved from one spot to another, as though she were in danger of losing her balance and falling. The queen, who was famous for her calm and stately demeanour; who had all the neighbouring chieftains in awe of her cool head, her intelligence and her dignity, was running about like a schoolgirl, practically giggling. Something, some magic potion or spell must have been at work, because this had happened so suddenly.

It had taken only one night of storytelling from the Trojan and the spell was cast. Iopas knew because one of the first things she did on the morning after the feast was arrange for the ceremonial bed in her chamber to be moved to the guest room. There had been objections. Anna, for one, was against it. She said: 'Why can't he sleep in the bed that's in there? The servants have enough to do, what with feeding and looking after these people, without beds being moved all over the place. There's nothing wrong with the bed in that room.'

'But my bed is the most beautiful thing in this whole palace, and I want Aeneas to have nothing but the best. The bedhead is carved from a single piece of wood by the most skilled woodworkers in the city. The mattress is as soft as a cloud. I want it moved into

Aeneas' room. We'll put the guest bed into my bed-chamber. Just while he's staying with us here.'

'Let us hope that his visit isn't too long then,' said Anna – and that made Dido furious, Iopas remembered. She'd stood in the corridor outside the guest room, almost spitting with fury.

'How can you say that? This is the first time I've had a chance to— Oh, never mind. But Aeneas is an honoured guest for as long as he cares to stay with us. Haven't you got work to do in the sewing room? I want the best linens for that room too. Will you see to that? Or do you object to him having decent bedclothes?'

Anna had muttered something under her breath and moved away. Iopas, knowing that his best chance of getting more information was talking to Anna, followed her into the sewing room. It was also possible that Elissa would be there, stitching or mending, and any glimpse of her made his day better. Because she was the queen's sister, Anna could hardly sit with the other young women who were constantly engaged in maintaining and refurbishing the hangings and fabrics that were the pride of the palace, but she'd made it her business to oversee what went on there, and to direct the work that the others were engaged in. She settled at a small table from which the other tables could be supervised and patted the chair beside her to indicate to Iopas that he could sit beside her.

The biggest table of all, which ran almost the whole length of the room, had an enormous length of purple-dyed cloth spread out on it. As well as the public hangings and linens, there was also the matter of the queen's garments. These had to be kept in perfect condition and new ones made at her request. Anna often said that her girls, as she called them, were the busiest workers in Carthage. They were young women with dainty fingers who had come from the surrounding villages to find work in the palace and now felt privileged to be working for their adored queen. The most gifted workers did the embroidery: the delicate flowers in silver and gold thread that edged Dido's clothes needed more care than routine mending and it was considered an honour to be given such work. Anna sometimes undertook this embroidery herself, and now she bent to unpick some stitches on a scarlet butterfly which had not turned out to her satisfaction. She said, 'That's one of the reasons I like this work.'

Iopas reflected that he hadn't mentioned embroidery. Anna continued, 'If something isn't right, you aren't forced to put up with it. You can change things. Make everything perfect. In real life, matters frequently run out of your control. That's what's happening now. With my sister.'

'In what way?' said Iopas, turning to face Anna and smiling his most winning smile. 'I know that all these arrangements have meant a lot of extra work for you. I saw how harassed you looked last night at the feast. I felt for you, truly.'

'You're a great comfort, Iopas. A great comfort. You appreciate what I do. I know that. And I didn't realize you were looking at me last night.'

Iopas decided to move the conversation on to something else before Anna was sidetracked into discussing his attention to how she looked. He said, 'You do so much. So many things that not everyone notices.'

Anna nodded vigorously. 'Exactly. Scarcely anyone *does* notice. But this latest thing – I don't know how that will turn out.'

'Latest thing?' The trick was to appear just interested enough to keep the confidences flowing and yet not so eager that the speaker was put on their guard. If Anna realized that she was giving him access to her private thoughts, she might quite suddenly stop talking. But he needn't have worried.

'She's falling in love with him. I can see it. She's been a stranger to love for so long that she's just plunged headlong into it, as if Love were a fountain and she dying of thirst. I could see it last night. She didn't take her eyes off him while he was talking. Did you see that?'

'Well, his stories enthralled us all, didn't they?'

'You had time to look elsewhere. You looked at me. You said so yourself.'

Back to that, Iopas thought. He said, 'But Queen Dido was sitting right beside him. It would have been impolite to look even a little bored. And no one could have been bored, hearing about the war in Troy. I could easily have listened for twice as long.'

'Hmm. Well, after you left, something happened. I saw . . . I'm not quite sure what I saw, but my sister was struck by Eros' arrow. That I'm completely sure of. For the first time since we arrived in Carthage she came to my room and sat on the end of my bed and went on and on about Aeneas and how handsome he was and how strong, and how much she longed to speak to him again, till I fell asleep while she was still in full flight. She woke me up a couple of times, but in the end she left me to sleep, and when I woke up this morning, what do I find but her moving the furniture from place to place to please him.'

'I'm sure Aeneas is most grateful for any hospitality. I think he would be perfectly satisfied with the bed in the guest bedroom.'

'Precisely! How well you understand things, for one so young! Aeneas has been tossed over the oceans in a wooden crate with no comforts or conveniences and the guest bedroom will be more luxurious than anything he imagined. No, it's Dido who will be pleased, and that means she loves him. She wants him to have the very best. I won't be surprised if she stretches herself out on top of the covers, as an added attraction.'

'Surely not!'

'No, perhaps not. But she's fallen for him. Even though she may deny it, I can tell.'

The door opened then, and Dido came into the sewing room. Iopas jumped up from where he'd been sitting, and the queen, smiling, settled herself next to Anna and put an arm around her shoulders.

'I'm sorry, Sister. I'm sorry for being so obstinate and for not listening to you when you were speaking nothing but the greatest sense.'

'What are you talking about? This isn't like you, Dido. You never admit I'm right – even though I often am, you know.'

'And I never admit I'm wrong, do I? Well, I am saying exactly that now. You're right about many things, and not least the matter of the bed. I was being stupid. My beautiful bed must, naturally, stay in my chamber and the guest bed will be fitted with a new mattress and be provided with the most splendid coverlet you can find. Are you satisfied?'

'Delighted,' Anna said, and Iopas wondered whether she'd be happy to leave things where they were – but no, she was going to say something more. 'How did you happen to change your mind?'

'Aeneas himself persuaded me. Oh, Anna, he's so thoughtful. When I told him of my plan, he said – and these are his exact, precise words, I promise you – *I wouldn't be able to sleep easily knowing that you had given up your bed for me. I assure you, the bed in the guest room provides me with more comfort than I need. More comfort than I've ever had, if I'm honest.* And do you know what the strange thing is, Anna?'

Anna shook her head. Dido continued: 'The amazing thing is, he's right. Of course it's unsuitable for me to give up my bed for a visitor. *Any* visitor. It's a matter of protocol. I am, after all, ruler in Carthage and I wouldn't want the court to see me accepting the second-best bed. It looks . . . well, it just doesn't look right.'

'No,' said Anna. 'I did try and tell you that.'

Iopas closed his eyes, readying himself for a barbed remark from the queen. Instead she said, 'Oh, you're my clever little sister, aren't you?' and planting a kiss on Anna's cheek, she sprang from the chair and ran out of the room like a joyful schoolgirl.

Anna smiled at Iopas and raised her eyebrows at him. He couldn't resist. He said, 'You were quite right as usual, Lady Anna. The queen is in love. No one could mistake it.'

Late in the night; the courtyard

'What I mainly remember from that time,' Iopas said, 'is your decision to keep the bed – this bed' – he nodded his head in the direction of the bed, which loomed up behind them – 'and how happy you were. I'd never seen you smiling so much before.'

Dido sighed. 'I've noticed something,' she said. 'While someone is using a piece of furniture, while you're sitting on your chairs or sleeping in your bed or eating off your tables, the item is beautiful. It's always useful, sometimes elegant – it might be a piece of wood that an artist has worked on for weeks in order to make it lovely – and then, when you decide that the item is no longer wanted, you move it somewhere to be got rid of. A courtyard or a rubbish dump, it doesn't make much difference. You've thrown it away for any number of reasons, and as soon as you do that it becomes no more than waste. Something you no longer want has turned in the blink of an eye from a treasure to a piece of garbage. That' – she pointed to the bed again, now piled high with cushions, clothes, pieces of armour, ornaments, even some toys which must have come from Ascanius' room – 'is just a bonfire waiting to happen.'

'No, surely not!' said Iopas. 'I hope you're speaking metaphorically, madam.'

'Go to your room now, Iopas, and thank you for your company. I am going back to my chamber. I don't want to sit out here any longer.'

'Let me walk with you then.' He got up and stood aside, and Dido, moved by the young man's care for her, touched him on the arm.

'That's kind of you, Iopas. I made a good decision when I chose you as my poet. And, Iopas' – she turned to him and spoke urgently – 'I want you to start thinking of an elegy. For – for Aeneas. He is leaving us tomorrow and I would like something to mark the day.'

'Certainly, madam. I will begin tonight. As soon as I am in my room.'

'No, wait till the morning. Things will be different then. Of that you may be sure.'

'Every day is unlike every other,' Iopas said, and they left the courtyard and began to walk together along the covered colonnade, where the torches were set in brackets on the walls, at such great distances one from the other that the flickering light cast many moving shadows everywhere. At the door of the small room in which Dido had chosen to hide, she left him, and Iopas watched the door closing behind her.

On his way to his own room he glimpsed a flash of silver in one of the recesses and stopped short. Could it have been a weapon? As he peered into the dimness and wondered what to do and whether he ought to call someone, he saw a white dog trotting down the corridor. A skinny hunting dog: that was what it seemed to be – and, yes, there it was, its paws clicking on the tiled floor. Who had come into the palace in the middle of the night with an animal? How did it get past the guards at the main gate? He was on the point of raising the alarm when someone spoke quite close to him and Iopas whirled round to see who it was.

'It's my dog,' said this person. She was a woman, slim and dressed in a silver tunic, holding a silver bow. She was very beautiful and Iopas noticed something strange about her face. It was marked with a trail of silver, as though she'd been weeping and her tears had dried to metal on her white skin.

'Who are you?' Iopas asked, whispering.

'Artemis,' said the young woman. 'Goddess of the Chase and Young Maidens.'

'What's your business with me?'

'None. I have come to see a young woman who serves the queen. No longer a maiden, alas. That is why I am weeping. I will leave the palace very soon, but I must see her.'

'Do you know her name?'

'No, but I will find her. She is very unhappy – but not as unhappy as Dido.'

'You know the queen?'

'Everyone, from the mountains to the coast, from the world of men to the heights of Olympus, knows who Dido is. And that she is bereft.'

'Can't you help her – if you are a goddess?'

'It is her fate. Even the Gods cannot change that. What is to be will be.'

Iopas watched the Goddess as she made her way along the corridor. By the time he reached his room he was wondering whether perhaps he'd been dreaming, even though this was not the first time he'd seen a goddess. But he was, after all, very tired. He'd been awake since just after dawn.

Elissa

The darkest time of the night; the maidservants' bedchamber

'I wish I could fall asleep,' Tanith said, snuffling into a square of cloth.

'I wish you would too,' said Nezral. 'That would allow us to get some rest.'

'Don't be so unkind!' Tanith sat up in bed and glared in the direction of Nezral's bed. 'I can't help being so unhappy. How can I sleep when I will never see Maron ever again? I'm unhappy, and if you were a proper friend, you'd sympathize with me and stop nagging me all the time.'

'Tell her, Elissa.' Nezral sighed loudly. 'Tell her I *am* a proper friend but I need some rest. We've been running around after the queen and I'm exhausted. I want to sleep, that's all. Keep your moaning and crying to the day time. That's what I mean. I'll be kinder in the morning, I promise.'

'We'll try and be a bit quieter,' said Elissa. 'Won't we, Tanith?'

Tanith said nothing, but turned to the wall. Nezral said, 'Don't sulk, Tanith. I'm very sorry about you and Maron, truly, but . . . Oh, it doesn't matter. I'm going to sleep. Goodnight to both of you.'

'Goodnight,' Elissa said, and from Tanith's bed came a kind of grunt. Nezral would have to be satisfied with that, Elissa thought.

She, too, was finding it hard to fall asleep. She lay with her eyes fixed on the ceiling for what seemed like a very long time. There was no sound in the palace, and at least Nezral was now asleep and snoring as she always did. Tanith was still snuffling and wiping her nose on a cloth. Elissa wondered idly how many such cloths she'd used up since Maron's departure. Luckily she worked in the laundry and would be able to wash them and hang them out to dry tomorrow. I can't cry, Elissa thought. I wish I could. Perhaps it would make me feel easier, happier. At the moment she felt as though her stomach were filled with hard stones, and her breasts were sore and she felt nauseous almost all the time. The baby. Their baby. Whenever her thoughts came back to the child, she found herself overwhelmed; incapable of grasping what this would mean. There are many moons before the birth, she told herself. Time enough to worry about the child later, when I've got over losing her father. *His* father . . . No, she was sure it was a girl she was carrying. She peered into the darkness, imagining what her and Aeneas' daughter might look like, and suddenly remembered the day Dido had dressed her up in royal finery.

Elissa had been in the palace for about a year when Anna sent her to the royal bedchamber with a newly finished dress for the queen.

'Come in, come in, child!' Dido smiled at her. She was sitting on a low stool beside an open chest. 'You've brought the new dress. Put it down over there, on the bed. Spread it out so that I can see it. Thank you.'

I did what she said as quickly as I could, Elissa thought, but I must have looked amazed at the splendour, because the queen laughed and said: 'You've never been in here, have you? Well, look around and sit down there and you can advise me on something.'

'I'll try,' Elissa had whispered, terrified that Dido's question would be impossible to answer.

'Don't be scared, Elissa. There's no right answer. It's a matter of opinion. At the banquet tonight I'm wearing this robe . . .' She pointed to a dress the colour of a living flame which she had draped over another seat.

'It's beautiful,' Elissa said.

'But what jewels do I wear with it? Emeralds? Coral . . . ? No, coral is quite the wrong colour. Too pale. Come, you can look through my jewel casket and help me choose.'

Dido stood up and took a box out of the chest in the corner of the chamber. She opened it and Elissa saw a tangle of gems and ornaments: brilliant amethysts and rubies, and opals glowing with a milky fire; topazes and turquoises, and something green and veined with black which she didn't recognize.

'I think . . . this,' she said. 'I don't know what it's called, but it's lovely.'

'Malachite,' said Dido. 'You're quite right. It will look magnificent.' She pulled out a string of round beads and laid them on the flame-coloured dress. 'See? You have a good eye, Elissa. And malachite is a stone that gives the wearer courage, so they say.'

And then, just as Elissa was about to return to her work, the queen called her back.

'D'you like dressing up? Did you do it when you were a little girl? Put on your mother's clothes and walk up and down pretending to be a lady? I did. I did it all the time, as if I were practising for the time when I'd be a queen in Carthage.'

Elissa blushed. 'No, lady. My mother . . . well, she didn't have very many clothes and we were always too busy on the farm.'

'Of course . . . I'm sorry. I should have thought. Then come here and let me dress you up now.'

'Now?'

'Wouldn't you like to?'

Elissa nodded, too overcome with joy to speak.

And then, she reflected, remembering that day now in the darkness and silence of her bed, the queen took off my dress and pulled a robe of white wool over my head and hung me with so many necklaces that I could only just hold my head up: a waterfall of gems spilling over my chest and hanging to my waist. She pulled bracelets on to my arms and put a garland of copper twisted into flowers on my head. And then she made me walk up and down while she clapped and laughed. I *did* feel like a princess for a while. Elissa turned over in the bed and faced the wall, remembering Dido's words that day. They had never left her.

'How proud your mother must be to have such a fine daughter . . . Well, now I'm proud of you too. Just as proud as any mother could be.'

And before I left the room she kissed me, Elissa thought. After I had taken off the clothes and jewels. Those days were long ago, and remembering them filled her with remorse. She had a duty to Dido and she'd failed in that duty. She should never have looked at Aeneas. She ought to have kept away from him. Elissa threw the covers back because the night was too warm. And now he's all I can think of, she told herself. Aeneas as he was when he first came to the palace. She closed her eyes and remembered the day when she'd gone with him and Dido down to the harbour. That, she thought, was the first time I realized that the two of them would love one another. That was the first time I really understood what jealousy meant.

'Go on, Elissa. She's waiting for you,' said Maron. 'My master says the queen particularly wants you in attendance today.'

'But what about Ascanius?' Elissa and the boy were in the garden, throwing and catching a painted ball made of the lightest wood. 'We're having a good time.'

'I'll play catch with you later, Ascanius,' said Maron. 'That'll be fun, right?'

'Elissa!' said the boy, and Elissa smiled.

'You see,' she said. 'He's used to me already.'

Maron said, 'That's true, but you've got to go where you're ordered. You can take over again when you get back from whatever it is the queen wants you for. Go on, she's waiting.'

Ascanius had settled down near a patch of earth and was busily building a fort with some pieces of broken tile.

'I can see why you're so anxious to be rid of me,' Elissa said. 'Tanith's coming, look . . .'

Maron smiled and said, 'I did tell her I'd be here in the garden. I suggested she might like to come and play with Ascanius. She seems very fond of him.'

'What are you two talking about?' said Tanith, hurrying over to where they were standing. She was pink in the face and Elissa wondered how much of that was caused by her almost running from the laundry and how much by her pleasure at the prospect of being alone with Maron.

She said, 'We've been talking about you, of course.'

'You haven't! Really? What did you say?' Tanith directed her question at Maron and he took her by the hand and said, 'If you come over here to this bench, I'll tell you. Come on.'

Tanith followed him quickly, turning her head towards Elissa as she went. She smiled in a way that meant: *I'll tell you what he says to me in our chamber tonight,* and the two of them disappeared to sit on a bench half hidden behind some shrubs in a pot.

'Don't forget you're supposed to be looking after Ascanius,' Elissa called.

'We won't,' Tanith called back, and Elissa could hear from her voice that she had been interrupted in the middle of kissing Maron. She smiled. How lucky Tanith was . . .

Elissa ran back into the palace. She'd been enjoying looking after Ascanius, but still, she was happy to think she'd been chosen specially by the queen, and of course, wherever Dido was, Aeneas would be there too, and this prospect made her stomach turn in a peculiar way, as though her guts were trembling and churning. How wonderful to be in his presence, even for a little while.

The queen had been busy since early morning. One of her handmaidens had already told Elissa that Dido wanted to create the impression that she'd taken no particular trouble with her toilet but always wore her hair in these curls and ringlets, bound with these ribbons, and that she was always dressed in such fine embroidered robes. The truth of it was (and this was how the handmaiden put it), 'The three of us had to take out almost every garment she possessed and spread them out over the bed so that the queen could decide. She chose a dress in a fabric that matched her eyes – she's out to enchant someone, that's for sure.'

Elissa found Dido and Aeneas in one of the shady rooms off the main courtyard. Mosaics patterned the marble floor and cushions were heaped on the low divans where the two of them were sitting, very close together.

'Thank you for coming, Elissa,' said Dido, smiling. 'We'll soon be going for a walk in the gardens and I would like you to accompany us. I've seen very little of you in the last few days. Sit there.' She pointed at a stool near the door and Elissa obeyed her at once.

'You won't be able to hear much from there,' said a voice in her ear, and Elissa, who had just sat down as commanded, nearly fell off the stool. Standing in the doorway was a tall, well-built woman, with white hair piled high on her head. She had piercing dark eyes, and carried a pomegranate in her hand. Her cloak was sewn with peacock feathers. Before Elissa could say a word, this person went on: 'I am Hera, the wife of Zeus, and it's thanks to me and Aeneas' mother, Aphrodite, that your mistress is so much in love with him. There are those who are against this union and they are powerful, but we will do our best. Listen . . . I will give your ears powers to hear what they say to one another and you will learn what love can be. You will be a witness. Be attentive.'

As Elissa stared at this apparition, the outlines of Hera's body began to blend into the marble walls and the only sign that the Goddess had been there was a peacock feather lying on the floor. As she picked it up and stroked it, wondering what she had seen, she realized that the Goddess had indeed touched her ears because suddenly she could hear every word that Dido and Aeneas were saying to one another.

'It's such a pleasure, Queen Dido,' she heard Aeneas say, 'to sleep ashore and not on a ship.'

Dido answered: 'It pleases me to hear that – and you've shaved your beard. Forgive me for making such a personal remark.'

'You have good servants who are skilful in the use of their implements, and after so many moons wandering at sea it's good to be rid of it. I feel . . . I feel cleaner.'

'You look like a youth now,' Dido said, and Elissa wondered how she could allow herself to speak thus to a man she had met so recently. The queen stood up and said to Aeneas: 'Let us go down to the city. It's such a beautiful morning and I did want to show it to you. Elissa, you will come with us in case I need anything.'

'Yes, lady,' Elissa said, and she followed Dido and Aeneas outside, still holding the peacock feather that Hera had dropped. They walked slowly through the garden, with Elissa two or three steps behind them.

'It's a beautiful garden,' Aeneas said. 'Many men must have worked hard to make it so.'

'They did. But come, I will show you my new buildings. The foundations are being laid for a theatre – if that would interest you.'

'Indeed it would.' Together they made their way towards the palace gates. From where they'd been standing, almost hidden behind trees and bushes, a few men emerged, carrying weapons. Aeneas smiled. 'I see your bodyguards are ready for us. Did you warn them they'd be needed?'

'No, they follow me wherever I go and I've grown so used to them that I scarcely notice they're there. They're well-trained.'

'Are you under any threat, Queen Dido?'

'I don't think so,' Dido answered. 'There are doubt-less those who would see me cast out and themselves ruling in my place, but they are unknown to me, and as long as I have the money in Carthage and the power, I don't feel myself menaced. On the contrary, I'm loved, I think. By most people. I've tried to be kind to those who work for me. I pay good money to the men who are building this city. One day, Aeneas, Carthage will be a power in the world.'

'I don't doubt it. And it would be hard not to love you . . . I mean, of course your people love you as their queen.'

They continued their progress through the city. He was blushing when Dido spoke to him. Elissa could see it even on his sunburned skin. Could it be that he means he loves the queen? She felt as though someone had dealt her a blow. I have no right to be jealous, she thought, but I can't help myself. Dido bent her head to acknowledge Aeneas' last remark and she was also blushing a little; then she turned to the Trojan and said, 'Tell me about yourself, Aeneas. What you didn't tell us at the banquet on your first night in Carthage. I'd like to know more about your wife.'

Aeneas went on walking, looking down at his feet. They'd arrived at the shore. 'May we sit somewhere? On that bench by the water?'

'Of course. This is the place I love best in the whole of Carthage. We can rest here for as long as you'd like to.' Dido raised her hand in a signal to the bodyguards, who took up their positions among the columns of the harbour-side buildings. 'Elissa, please sit down over there.' The queen pointed to a low wall. 'You'll be in the shade.'

'Yes, lady,' Elissa said, and went to sit where she'd been told. She stroked the peacock feather and then threaded it into her garments, weaving it in and out of the loose-woven fabric of her dress. Amazingly, she could still hear every word the queen and Aeneas were saying to one another. Hera was truly a powerful goddess.

'Creusa was not the person I thought I would wed,' said Aeneas. 'There was a young woman I loved when I was a boy, but my father chose Creusa for me and my love for her grew after I married her. That sometimes happens, doesn't it?'

'It does. It happened to me. My husband, Sychaeus, was ten years older than me and I was frightened to find myself a wife while I was not much more than a child. But Sychaeus was so kind and gentle to me that I became fond of him; I only realized how much I loved him when he was killed. Because of the sorrow I felt whenever I thought of him.'

'Creusa was a good woman, and her son, Ascanius, is the person I love most in the whole world. I remember her with gratitude and reverence, but so much has happened since she died that sometimes I can't call her to mind and I feel unworthy. I find it hard to picture her face. She's no longer present to me and that makes me sad.'

'If you talk of her often, to her son and to others, like me' – Dido was speaking very gently and soothingly – 'that will ensure that she is not forgotten.'

'My mother says that love is the most important thing in the world.'

'Tell me about her. About your mother.'

What a lot of questions Dido was asking! She must be very interested in Aeneas to be so eager to know every single thing about him, Elissa thought. Every tiny detail of his life, his past, his relations, was fascinating to her. It's fascinating to me too, Elissa reflected, but he'd never speak to me in the way he speaks to Dido.

'My mother is Aphrodite, the Goddess of Love.'

Dido was staring at him, and even Elissa found it hard not to exclaim aloud. The queen said: 'Your mother is a goddess?'

Aeneas nodded. 'She is. And there are other Gods who have my future in their hands. Zeus himself has me in his care. And Hera too is interested in my fate. What I say sounds boastful and, because I have no more than a few men and three ships, also a little mad.'

'Tell me,' Dido said, and Elissa saw her touch him on the arm briefly, as if to encourage him.

'I'm to found a dynasty – there, across the ocean. It will be a power in the world. It sounds ridiculous, I know.'

'Not at all,' Dido said, but then she was silent for a long time. At last she went on: 'I understand very well the desire to rule. I share it. I'm proud of this city and

126

my happiness is bound up with its prosperity and the welfare of its people.'

'You are the perfect queen,' Aeneas said, and offering Dido his arm again, he stood up. 'Will you come back to the palace with me now? I have to ensure that my men have been settled in their accommodation.'

'How thoughtless I am!' said Dido, standing up at once. 'We'll go back as quickly as possible. I wish you'd told me earlier. I'm sorry. I've taken my time . . .'

'It's been a pleasure, my lady.'

'Please call me Dido,' she said. 'And I will call you Aeneas, if you allow it.'

'You didn't need to ask.'

'I like to know where I stand.'

Elissa saw Aeneas turn so that he and Dido were facing one another. He put his hands on her upper arms, and for a wild moment she thought the two of them were going to embrace, and even kiss one another. Elissa saw the queen blushing again, and Aeneas' gaze didn't move from her face.

'You stand high in my estimation,' he said. 'I'm your friend for ever. I have . . . I admire you more than I can say. You knew that, didn't you?'

Dido nodded, and they started to make their way back to the palace, with Elissa following them. The queen didn't say a word as they walked and Aeneas kept looking sideways at her. Elissa wondered what could be wrong, because it had been quite clear, up to a moment ago, that Dido was more than friendly towards Aeneas. At last, as they stepped out of the sunlight and into the cool colonnades, the Trojan said: 'You're silent, Dido. What are you thinking about?'

'Nothing of any interest, Aeneas, I assure you. Thank you for your company. I have enjoyed walking with you.'

'And I with you,' Aeneas said, and bending low over Dido's hand, he kissed it before walking away.

Dido stared at the place where his mouth had been for a long time. Then she came to herself, and turning to Elissa, said: 'I'm sorry to have taken you from your duties, Elissa. You may return to them now.

'Yes, lady,' Elissa said, and went to find Ascanius.

The night edging nearer to the dawn; the maidservants'
bedchamber

How can I be dreaming, Elissa thought, if I'm not asleep? She was in her bed but she could tell she was awake because there were Tanith and Nezral and she could hear them breathing deeply. Nezral was making the kind of noise you'd call a snore if you weren't a good friend of hers. Or could it be that both her companions were part of the dream as well? Maybe she *was* asleep, because all at once she became aware of a noise like a dog panting. There were no dogs in the palace. Cats padded along the corridors and lurked in the shadows, but they were needed as mouse-catchers. Dogs were only used for hunting and were kept firmly

128

out of doors in kennels near the stables. Besides, no dog she'd ever seen looked like this one. He was white, with fur that seemed almost to gleam, and his eyes were like translucent chips of amber. Elissa struggled to sit up and blinked in amazement.

'Oh, you lovely creature!' she whispered. 'Where did you come from?' She pushed back the sheet, went to kneel beside the animal and began to stroke him. 'You're beautiful. Where is your owner? What are you doing by my bed?'

'He's my dog. And I've come to speak to you, Elissa.'

'Who are you?' As Elissa peered into the darkness, a silvery shape stepped away from the shadow of the wall. 'How did you get past the guards?'

'I am Artemis, the Goddess who protects young girls. Also the Goddess of the Hunt. And of Childbirth. He is one of my hunting dogs. Guards mean nothing to me. They never see me.'

A goddess! Elissa stared at the woman and noticed that her tunic was shimmering as though it were made of beaten silver; that her hair was the colour of moonlight; that she was crying. The tears falling on to her cheeks were silver too.

'Why are you weeping?'

'I'm weeping for you. You're no longer a maiden. You are going to bear a child. This is the end of your youth. You have thrown away the gift of your love. Aeneas did not deserve what you gave him.'

'But I loved him! I still love him, and that's not going to change, ever. I don't regret what happened. I don't regret this child that is growing inside me. How can I be sad about that?'

'You will find out,' Artemis said, 'that the pain of bearing the child is only the beginning. Do you know what it means to be a mother? You are tied for ever to another person. You can never be free. The child you bear is bound to you for ever.'

'No, it's not,' Elissa said, struggling to keep from crying herself. She got up from the hard floor and sat down on her bed. How did this Goddess dare to come and tell her such sad things! Wasn't Aeneas fleeing Carthage enough to make her miserable? In any case, it wasn't true. Elissa frowned and wondered if she dared to contradict an inhabitant of Olympus. She said, 'Mothers and children are not always bound together. I've left my own mother. I hardly ever think of her now.' Was that true? Well, maybe not, but Elissa didn't care.

'She thinks of you.'

'No she doesn't. She has the other children to worry about, and my father too. She has no time to fret about me.'

'You know nothing. You are always in her mind.'

'That's not true! You're lying. You're just . . . You're put out because I'm no longer a virgin. That's something you don't like and you're taking your anger out on me.'

Artemis shook her head. 'No, child. I'm not angry with you. I am regretful. I foresee much anguish, but it does no good to be angry. And you will find out the truth of what I've told you when you're a mother your-self. The ties of the flesh bind you for ever. You'll see.'

'Did you come to warn me? To scold me? To comfort me? I don't understand.'

'You don't need to understand. You're a mortal. I have seen you. I have spoken to you. You now know what to expect.'

'I don't. I don't know what to expect. Tell me. If you've come to warn me, then warn me properly.'

'Dido . . . Take care, Elissa, in your dealings with the queen.'

Elissa stared at Artemis as she spoke. She was on the point of asking what that meant; how was she supposed to take care? Should she leave the palace? And then someone else was speaking in the room. She turned her head and saw that the dark sleeping shapes of Nezral and Tanith hadn't moved. Amber light filled the chamber and Elissa caught sight of Aphrodite, standing in the doorway.

'Don't disturb yourself, child,' said the Goddess of Love. 'I've come to speak with Artemis. She and I are in disagreement about something. Be silent.'

Artemis said, 'I'm angry, Aphrodite, and I won't deny it. You've been unkind to this child. Not only did you make her fall in love with someone who could never return her devotion; you also knew that her mistress was in love with Aeneas and yet you couldn't stop yourself. You meddled. You're forever meddling.'

'You call it that,' said Aphrodite, 'but you don't understand love, Artemis. Why should you, being the

131

Goddess of all maidens? The pain of love is a price worth paying for the glory that comes with it. That's my opinion.'

'And mine is that the misery love brings is enough to keep anyone a maiden for ever. Look at this child. She's going to be a mother and you are as much to blame for that as the man who lay with her.'

'What can you possibly know about the pleasures of being a mother?' said Aphrodite. 'You are a maiden. But I have a child: Aeneas, my beloved son. That love, of a mother for her child, is worth any amount of pain. Any amount.'

'You say I am a maiden and don't understand such matters,' said Artemis, 'but I am also the Goddess of those who attend births, so I know what I'm talking about far better than you. The agonies of childbirth, if the baby survives, are simply the beginning. For the rest of the mother's life she shares her offspring's every sorrow, every bruise and cut and illness, every disappointment, every dark mood. And how many die in infancy? Very many. Too many. That pain is with the mother till she goes down to the kingdom of Hades.'

'Pah!' Aphrodite's exasperation was plain. 'What about the joys? The pleasure in every success? The unending love that a mother and child feel for one another, the pride in your child's achievements?'

'Nothing compared to the pain. Nothing. The pleasure is soon forgotten. The sorrow is not. That remains. And there are mothers and children whose love is more like hatred – do you consider that?'

'Ask her,' Aphrodite said. 'Ask this girl. Would she rather be pregnant or not? I know her answer.'

'I won't ask, because it's happened and it's the will of the Gods – well, *your* will, Aphrodite – and all I can do is comfort her. That's why I came.'

'Oh, really? I thought it was to pick a fight with me. Then you can spare yourself the trouble, Artemis. I am the one who is here to comfort her.'

'Nonsense. It's you who's picking a quarrel with me, but I know why you're really here. It's for Dido. To see what a pass she has come to – as a result of your wishes.'

Aphrodite sank down on to the chair just inside the doorway. 'I cannot deny it. Perhaps I do *somewhat* regret what has happened to Dido. I could see that my son was attracted and it's hard to deny a child something you can easily give him. And it was difficult to resist Hera, who encouraged the love between them even while she knew very well that his destiny was to leave Carthage for ever.'

'You spoil Aeneas. That's another danger of motherhood, isn't it? Anything he fancied, you tried to give him. Isn't that right?'

'I don't regret it. I never regret anything. Regret is for weaklings. Mortals must submit to their fate, that's all.'

'Yes,' said Artemis, and turning to Elissa, she said, 'Be comforted. When your time comes to give birth, I'll attend you. Don't be frightened.'

'I'm not,' Elissa whispered, but she was lying. She

had seen what her mother went through giving birth to her brothers and sisters, and dreaded that pain, but if the Goddess would help her, then surely her child would come quickly and easily into the world? She resolved to pray to Artemis in future, for a swift delivery. Now the Goddess laid a cool silver hand on her brow and said: 'Sleep now. We will leave you.'

Elissa climbed into her bed and lay back on her pillows, and the fragrance of almond blossom and roses filled the room as Aphrodite left the bedchamber. The dog's paws clicked as he trotted away, and the silver light that surrounded Artemis faded to a darkness broken only by the flickering of a torch a long way down the corridor.

Cubby

The night edging nearer to the dawn; the courtyard

Cubby wasn't sure if he'd been asleep or not. He'd just had a dream and it wasn't like any other dream he could remember. The more he thought about it, the less he could bring it back to his mind, but there was a dog in it, and a kind of silver person, and they were running along the dark corridor. Oh well, Cubby thought. I don't suppose it meant anything in particular. He was a bit disappointed to find himself dropping off every now and then. The master of the guard didn't say in so many words, but surely he meant Cubby to stay awake so that he could deal with anyone who wanted to interfere in any way with the stuff that belonged to the queen.

He'd got quite used to the size of the bed. At first it seemed to take up more space than any piece of furniture he'd ever seen before, but now it looked normal: the right size for Queen Dido at any rate. She'd been here a while ago, and had sent him to stand further away while she chatted to that long-haired chap who had a bit of a girlish look. Iopas, they called him. Cubby had never spoken to him before tonight, but had seen him wandering around the palace. Seemed like a bit of a weed, with skinny arms and legs. Maron liked him though, so he couldn't be all bad. It was true that Cubby was hurt sometimes that Maron chose to spend more time with Iopas than with him. Still, he told himself, I'm nothing but a kitchen boy and I'm lucky that Maron spoke to me at all.

It was very quiet now and that made Cubby feel nervous. He didn't really like silence. The thing about it was, you kept thinking you heard something in the nothing that you were actually hearing. He shook his head. This was complicated and it made his head hurt just to think such things. Up until a while ago, the courtyard had been quite noisy, even though it was night time. The servants who brought the stuff to put on the bed didn't exactly keep their voices down. Cubby didn't try to keep track of the weapons and clothes and bedclothes and odds and ends they'd piled up on the mattress, but after they'd gone he went and had a bit of a nose around and found something that he really liked. It was a toy crocodile on wheels.

Cubby looked around to make sure no one was looking and then picked up the toy. I remember this, he thought. That kid – what was his name? Ascanius, that's right – this is his toy. Why's he left it here? Can't be that he doesn't want it any longer. He really loved it. He came racing into the kitchen with it, and I was there and not working for a change. Cubby held the little crocodile in his hands and suddenly felt sad. Well, the kid must have gone now and left this behind. It was a shame. When he'd burst into the kitchen (it wasn't so long ago, either), he had the crocodile tucked under one arm and he was waving a wooden sword about with his other hand. Cubby sat down with his back against the bedstead and thought himself back to that day.

For once the kitchen was quiet and there was no one about. Cubby wondered whether he ought to make a start on preparing the vegetables for the evening meal when suddenly he heard a high-pitched yelling sound and a small boy ran into the room at high speed, almost bumping into Cubby as he went.

'Hello, little boy,' Cubby said. 'What's the rush?'

'I'm not little. I'm big. I'm Ascanius,' the boy said, coming to a halt just by the table. Then, 'What's your name?'

'They call me Cubby.'

'That's a funny name,' said Ascanius. 'Why do they call you that?'

'I used to live in a cupboard when I was small.'

'People don't live in cupboards,' said the little boy, sounding very definite about it. Then he looked a little worried and added, 'Do they?'

'Not a lot of people,' said Cubby, 'but I did.'

The boy started laughing. He said, 'Cubby – that's funny. My crocodile's name is Croccy.'

'Right.' Cubby nodded in agreement. 'That makes sense.'

'D'you want to pull him? You can pull him.'

'Yeah, all right.' Cubby took the string from the little boy's hand and walked around the kitchen with the wooden creature rattling along on the hard floor behind him. He felt a fool, and a bit sad too. He'd never had a family, or none that he could remember, and he wasn't very good at playing because no one had ever played any kind of game with him. His first memory was of this very kitchen. He must have been brought here – dumped here – when he was tiny. His mother. His father. He must have had one of each, even if he never knew them, and he might also have had some brothers and sisters but they'd obviously decided that they didn't want him in their house. The kitchen workers had been kind to him for the most part, and Cubby could remember being allowed to bang on lids with wooden spoons and splash in basins of dirty water after the dishes had been washed. It hadn't been such a bad childhood and at least he'd always had enough to eat. Still, he could never join in with any conversations about home, like the other kitchen lads. He couldn't tell any stories about where he'd come from.

This used to worry and upset him when he first came here, but he'd been young. Now that he was older and bigger he'd stopped thinking about home altogether, most of the time. It was only seeing this toy and this little boy when he wasn't really expecting it – that made him a bit sad, gave him a kind of sore feeling just above his stomach. It was so strange to him, the pain, that he stood there staring at the crocodile and Ascanius, wondering whether he'd eaten something that didn't agree with him, but no. The pain left him gradually, and Cubby went back to playing with the child.

'Oi, Cubby, whatcha think you're doing?' That was Cook, who'd come back into the kitchen. 'Time you were putting those lambs on the spit or no one will get any food tonight. Jump to it, boy! Who's this? Don't want kids in here, thank you very much. And what's this bloody toy doing under my feet? This is a kitchen, not a bleeding nursery.'

Then Cook bent down, picked up the crocodile and thrust it into Ascanius' arms. 'Scat!' he yelled, putting his huge red face very near the boy's. 'And also scram. Don't want to see you in here ever again, d'you hear?'

'I'll take him back.' Cubby surprised himself by speaking out, even though he wasn't in the habit of addressing Cook directly. It was better to stay out of his way if at all possible. 'I'll go with him to his nursemaid. I know where she is. Come on, Ascanius.'

He tried to take the child's hand, but Ascanius pulled away and began to run through the corridors. Cubby wasn't very good at running but he shuffled along behind him as quickly as he could. And there was Maron, standing in the doorway of the nursery.

'Ascanius!' he cried. 'We've been looking for you everywhere. Where have you been?' He caught sight of

Cubby and said to him, 'Hello, Cubby. Has he been bothering you in the kitchen? I'm sorry if he has. It's hard to keep an eye on him every minute. He's always running away.'

'No problem, Maron,' said Cubby, blushing. Maron always spoke to him as though they were the best of friends. 'We had a nice game, didn't we? But Cook said we had to go.'

'I've got a sword!' Ascanius shouted, and began to flourish his wooden sword at Cubby, who parried with his hands. Soon the two of them were dancing around the corridor in a mock fight, with the child laughing and Cubby trying hard not to appear too clumsy and heavy-footed. He was already out of breath, but Maron was smiling so he was happy to continue with the game.

'Who's your opponent?' said a low voice, and there was Aeneas. They stopped moving, and Ascanius brought his sword to rest just a hair's breadth away from Cubby's stomach.

'Give up!' Ascanius shouted. 'Surrender!'

'I give up!' Cubby said, putting his hands above his head.

Ascanius ran to his father, who gathered him up and held him.

'I'm sorry if my son's been worrying you,' Aeneas said. Cubby couldn't get over it. This was the prince from Troy. Everyone knew that the queen was in love with him and some said he might become the next king of Carthage. He'd overheard the queen's sister, Anna, moaning about how difficult it was for anyone to speak to Dido these days because she was so taken up with the Trojan. And now this person was speaking to him. For a moment Cubby couldn't think what to say. First Maron and now his master. In the end he muttered, 'I liked playing with your son, sir.'

'And I'm sure he enjoyed playing with you. Say goodbye to this kind lad, Ascanius.'

'Bye!' the child shouted. 'Bye, Cubby!'

'Don't be so rude, boy! Cubby's not a proper name!' Aeneas chided him, and Cubby hurried to say: 'No, it's all right, sir. That's what I'm called. Everyone calls me Cubby.'

'Do they?' Aeneas looked solemn for a moment and then grinned. 'Very well. Thank you, Cubby.'

Cubby stood and watched as Aeneas, still carrying his son, went into the nursery to find Elissa. Maron said, 'You were really good with him, Cubby. Thanks. He's a bit of a handful for Elissa sometimes and I'm grateful for any bit of help with childcare. See you later!' He walked down the corridor and Cubby gazed after him, wondering where he was going. Other people always seemed to have things to do and places to go to. My place is the kitchen, Cubby thought, and I'd better get back there now before Cook comes looking for me.

The night edging nearer to the dawn; the courtyard

Cubby sighed as he remembered that day and put the

141

wooden crocodile back on top of the other toys and clothes heaped on the royal bed. It wobbled there for a moment and then fell down on to the flagged stones of the courtyard with a noise that startled Cubby so much he nearly jumped out of his skin. He looked around, hoping that the racket wouldn't have woken anyone, and after listening for a bit he reckoned he'd got away with it. The silence was complete and Cubby sat down again. After a while his head lolled down on to his chest and he began to dream. No, I mustn't fall asleep, he told himself, lifting his head up again. I'm a guard.

Just then he heard a funny noise. At first he couldn't think what it was: a sort of rhythmic clicking sound, exactly as if a dog were trotting about on the tiled floor. He was back: the dog from his dream. He looked up and couldn't believe what he was seeing. There *was* a dog, but it wasn't any old mutt, and certainly not an animal he'd ever seen the like of before. This creature had a silvery coat, long, droopy ears, a long pointed nose and thin legs. A girl was walking along behind it, and she was dressed in a short silver tunic and carried a silver bow. He'd never seen her before in his life, and however much he admired her dog and however pretty she was, Cubby was fairly certain that strangers weren't meant to be traipsing the corridors in the middle of the night.

'*Oi!*' he shouted, remembering just after he'd said it that he was supposed to say, *Who goes there?* Perhaps it wasn't too late to speak, even now, but the words wouldn't come.

'Don't be concerned,' said the woman. He could see, now that she was a little closer to him, that she was older than she looked, though he wouldn't have been able to say how old exactly. 'I've just come from Elissa's room.'

'Oh, righty-o!' Cubby said, and the silver woman drifted off down the corridor. He looked for the dog, but that had disappeared as well. Never mind, he told himself. It's too late to ask her what her name is. Elissa will tell me in the morning. I'm not chasing down the corridors and leaving this bed unguarded. No way.

Elissa

'What's the matter, Elissa?' Nezral mumbled. 'Are you
sick again?'

'No, no, I'm not. I'm sorry. It must have been a
dream. I didn't mean to wake you.'

Nezral sighed and turned over and went back to
sleep almost at once. Elissa went on sitting on her bed,
staring into the darkness. I'm not going to sleep now,
she thought. And I'm hungry. I want something salty
to eat. She picked up a thin cotton robe and pulled it
on over her nightgown. Did she dare to walk along the
corridors to the kitchen in the middle of the night?
Yes, of course she did. What harm could possibly come
to her? It was true that tonight of all nights, when there
were guards everywhere and half the palace servants
hadn't gone to bed just in case the queen decided she
wanted something, she was sure to be noticed, but so
what? A person was allowed to be hungry in the middle

144

of the night, weren't they? If anyone sees me, I'll tell them I'm going to get something to eat, which is no more than the truth.

She tiptoed through the silence, and as she passed the courtyard, glanced at Cubby and couldn't help smiling. He'd fallen asleep, leaning against one of the legs of the queen's bed, and if the idea was that he should be guarding it, it wasn't working very well. Elissa didn't know why Dido had brought the bed to the courtyard, nor why a guard was necessary, but presumably it was to stop the servants and even some of the courtiers helping themselves to Aeneas' possessions. For a moment Elissa wondered whether she dared to go over to the bed and perhaps take something as a keepsake. No, she told herself. I can't. If I'm caught, they'll throw me out of the palace. Dido will never forgive me.

I'm a fool, she told herself, tiptoeing down the stairs that led to the main corridor. I'm carrying his child – I'm hardly likely to forget him. I don't need a souvenir.

Elissa walked especially quietly as she passed the room in which Dido had hidden herself. There was someone playing a lyre. Where was the music coming from? And who would dare to play in the middle of the night and risk disturbing the queen, when everyone knew she was in a terrible state? Sounds carry strangely at night and it didn't take long for Elissa to realize that the music was coming from Dido's room. The door was slightly open and she pushed it a little and caught sight of the queen herself, sitting on the bed with her legs crossed and a lyre resting on her knees. She had her back to the door and was plucking the strings and humming to the music.

'Oh! I'm sorry, my lady. I didn't realize . . .' The tune was plaintive, and made Elissa feel like weeping, and when Dido turned round, she saw that the queen's own cheeks were wet with shed tears.

'What can I do?' she asked, coming into the room and approaching the bed. 'Should I send for your sister?'

'Nothing, Elissa. Don't do anything. Don't fetch anyone. I want to be left alone. I'm . . .' Dido put aside the lyre, and bringing her knees up to her chin, she clung to them, with her face half hidden, rocking backwards and forwards and sobbing, the sounds of her sorrow muffled but still loud in the dimly lit room. A small torch above the doorway was the only source of light, and Dido's shadow loomed black on the wall behind her.

'Come and sit beside me, Elissa. Tell me something cheerful.'

How can I, Elissa thought, when my heart is aching so? She said, 'I think it's a sad day for all of us, lady.'

'This is what happens, you see? I've stopped thinking about anyone else. I should've understood that you'd be unhappy. Little Ascanius – I know how devoted you were to that boy. You must be missing him dreadfully. Poor Elissa! Come and sit beside me and we'll share our pain.'

Dido patted the mattress and Elissa came and

perched on the edge of the bed, nervous of being so close to the queen, though she looked nothing like a ruler now. Elissa saw a woman wearing creased garments, with her hair dishevelled, smelling a little stale, as though she'd forgotten to wash herself. It was hard sometimes to remember that even queens, however grand and beautiful they were, were made like other women, and seeing Dido in this state made Elissa feel doubly sad. She was reminded of her own mother, who frequently had no time to bathe and found something to weep about almost every day.

'Do you remember,' she began, trying to think of something amusing to tell the queen, 'the day when Ascanius fell in the fishpond? How angry Aeneas was with him and how funny he looked, sitting in the water with a fish flapping about in his hand? He didn't want to let it go, and he started crying when I made him put it back. I felt so terrible . . . It was my duty to see that he kept away from the water. I thought Aeneas would shout at me for my neglect of his son, but he was laughing too and said it wasn't my fault and it would take a god with a thousand eyes to make sure Ascanius kept out of mischief.'

Elissa glanced to her left and saw that Dido's eyes were closed. She was leaning against the wall and seemed calmer. Perhaps she was falling asleep. Elissa made up her mind to wait and see what the queen did next. She settled herself more comfortably on the bed and allowed her thoughts to return to that day – the day Ascanius fell into the fish pond.

*   *   *

Elissa realized, within a few days of starting to look after Ascanius, that she'd never played before. In the countryside, small children were workers on the land, helpers in the kitchen, and set to perform all kinds of tasks as soon as they could walk and grasp something in their hands. She tried to think back to what she and her brothers and sisters used to do in their free time and came to the conclusion that there wasn't any to speak of. By the time the work was done; by the time her mother put out the evening meal, she and the others were exhausted, and Elissa remembered many evenings when her father would have to pick up the sleeping younger children before the food was eaten and take them to their beds.

When Dido asked her to look after Ascanius, Elissa had said yes with pleasure. He was a smiling, talkative child, and on his first night in Carthage, when she put him to bed, he was happy to lie there and listen to her singing the songs of her own childhood. These weren't lullabies, but melodies her mother used to sing as she worked. Still, they served their purpose and Ascanius had fallen asleep at once. Elissa thought at the time: This is easy. I'm going to enjoy looking after him. I'll be let off other work too. She was pleased about this for the most part, though she knew she'd miss the occasions when Dido called her to help with doing her hair or choosing her jewels or taking her clothes to the sewing room to be mended. But no one knew how long the Trojans would be staying in the city and she could go back to her normal duties when they left.

She soon discovered how different looking after a small child was from any other work in the whole world. There were no tasks, either domestic or agricultural, for Ascanius to perform, and therefore it fell to Elissa to entertain the boy, which would have been pleasant for a few hours but became burdensome and irritating if you had to do it all day long. Dido had set her woodcarvers to work at once and within a few days the child had been given an army of wooden soldiers, a crocodile mounted on wooden wheels which he could pull along by a leather thong, a shield and sword, and many bricks with which to build imaginary forts. The crocodile in particular was a favourite and became any creature Ascanius wanted him to be. Often he was the wooden horse which had been taken into Troy and from which the Greek soldiers had leaped, ready to burn the city to the ground.

'Who told you this story, Ascanius?' Elissa asked when they first played the game. She had to lie stretched out on the tiled floor and push the crocodile through the gate that she'd helped the child build from wooden blocks.

'Maron told me,' said Ascanius. 'He said my daddy fought with the horse. He killed the horse.'

'I see,' said Elissa. The boy was obviously a bit muddled about what had actually happened, but was quite happy with his version of the Trojan War, where a crocodile went mad among the bricks and brought

149

them tumbling down on top of himself. This made Ascanius laugh and roll about on the floor, and Elissa was happy to join in with him.

But even after playing with the bricks and with the soldiers; even taking into account giving him his food and putting him to bed, there were still long stretches of the day which had to be filled. Tentatively, Elissa suggested to Dido that they might go outside some-times, to the garden. They could, she suggested, perhaps sit by the fishpond and admire the fish.

'Of course,' Dido said. 'You can go wherever you like. Keep to the grounds of the palace, but yes, little boys do like to run around. I should have thought of it. I'm not used to considering the needs of children.'

And so Elissa and Ascanius fell into the habit of going down to the garden every afternoon. Sometimes Maron came with them, and though it ought to have been easier with him to help her, he was very often taken up with chatting to Tanith, who seemed miraculously able to have free time to be with him in the garden when others were working. The two of them would disappear behind a tree, or sit on a well-shaded bench, and while giggles and cries sometimes came to Elissa on the breeze, for the most part she forgot about them and had to deal with Ascanius by herself. She didn't begrudge her friend these happy times but often wished it could have been her and Aeneas instead, and then chided herself for her stupidity. What would Aeneas be doing with her? It was only in her imagination that the two of them could be together.

While Elissa sat on a bench in the shade of the palm trees, the little boy ran around the flowerbeds, lined up stones in patterns and stood at the edge of the ornamental pond and admired the fish. She'd noticed that Iopas was often visible at one of the windows that looked on to the garden while she was out there, and she couldn't help smiling to herself whenever she saw him. Sometimes she lifted her hand and waved to him, which led quite often to him vanishing away altogether, as if he were embarrassed to be caught staring at her. She had no real interest in him, whatever his feelings were for her. Still, it was gratifying to be admired. Sometimes she pretended she hadn't seen him and deliberately turned away from the palace and concentrated on the fish in the pond, and that meant, she knew, that Iopas would be there all the time she wasn't looking in his direction. Ascanius had given the fish names like Hector, Paris and Troilus, and there was even one, a particularly enormous dark creature with silver markings on its back, which he called Odysseus, after the main enemy of the Trojans.

Then one day Ascanius fell into the pond. It happened because Elissa's mind was on other things. She'd been distracted by Tanith, who was on her way back to her work in the laundry after a pleasant time with Maron. He had already left the garden and gone into the palace.

'I just had to tell you,' she said. 'They're saying things in the laundry about Dido. She's spending every spare minute with Aeneas apparently, and not paying attention to matters of state. All kinds of people come and wait for her to give her judgement on different matters or choose things or make decisions, and she isn't there. She's walking about in the city with Aeneas. She's moony-eyed about him. Any fool can see that.'

'She's just being polite, that's all. He's a guest.'

'You're naïve, Elissa. We've had guests before. No one's ever had this treatment. And you've seen her looking at him, haven't you? Tongue hanging out.'

Elissa said nothing about her own feelings for Aeneas. Tanith could be very uncouth sometimes. She'd also be quick to spread what she said to everyone in the palace, and more would be made of her words than she intended. 'Well, he's very handsome, isn't he?' she ventured at last. 'And he's nice.'

'Have you spoken to him?'

'Not properly, but of course when he comes and kisses Ascanius goodnight, and some other times too. He says hello. And goodbye. Not more than that, no.'

She didn't add: *And when he does speak to me, my stomach turns over.* She hadn't even admitted to herself that one of the reasons she was so careful to be nice to Ascanius was in the hope that his father would notice her and thank her and come to depend on her. She would have died rather than admit her most secret daydreams, in which she and Aeneas and Ascanius were a real family, with herself sitting at the head of the table and presenting delicious food to her husband and child. And her most private and hidden fantasies were kept for the night, and Elissa didn't even like to think about those while the sun was shining. During the daylight hours, if her mind strayed to them, she would find herself blushing and try hard to think of something else.

'Where's Ascanius?' Tanith asked. 'He's such a sweetie. I want a cuddle from that lovely little boy before I go back to work.'

Elissa looked around. 'Ascanius? Where are you? Are you hiding?' She felt herself grow cold. She'd been talking to Tanith and not attending to the child. She stood up and began to walk towards the pond. 'Show me where you are, you naughty boy! This isn't a game, Ascanius. I'm serious. Show yourself!'

Suddenly Ascanius appeared on the far side of the pond, standing on the marble rim, balancing on it and looking far from steady on his feet. Elissa started to run. She shouted out: 'Don't move, Ascanius. Don't move, I'm coming to get you.'

As she ran, it occurred to her to wonder how on earth he'd managed to get up there. The rim of the basin was quite high. Surely too high for a small child to reach? She was too late. He was in the water and crying gleefully: 'Look at me, Elissa! Look at me! I'm going to catch a fish!'

'*Oh!* Ascanius! I told you and told you. That's a pond for fish. Now you're all wet and dirty too. What's your father going to say?'

'His father will say: *Naughty, silly boy!*' Aeneas and Dido had appeared suddenly. Where from? They must have been on their way down to the pond and she

153

hadn't noticed that either. Now there was no chance of her getting the child out of the pond and dry and dressed before his father had caught her out in such neglect. Perhaps, Elissa thought frantically, he'll say I mustn't look after Ascanius any more. Perhaps—

'Not your fault, Elissa,' Aeneas said, trying to reach his son, who was still enjoying himself in the water and seemed to have seized one of the inhabitants of the basin in both hands.

'Look, Father!' he shouted. 'I've caught a fish! It's Odysseus. That's his name.'

Aeneas, Dido and Ascanius all burst out laughing. Elissa, now that she understood she wasn't going to be in trouble, joined in tentatively.

'Come out of there now, son,' said Aeneas. 'We've had a good time laughing but it's time to go inside now. Time to get you out. Drop that fish and come here so that I can lift you out of the water.'

'Don't want to!' said Ascanius, frowning and looking as though he was prepared to fight to stay in the cool of the pond. 'Want to stay here.'

'I'm not discussing this,' said Aeneas. 'I said, enough, didn't I? Just get yourself over to the edge here and I'll give you a piggyback all the way to your room.'

Ascanius sat tight in the middle of the pond, though his grin was now a bit uncertain. Elissa, who had been wondering how he'd managed to climb up to the edge of the basin, saw that he'd piled a few stones into a kind of little tower. Cheeky monkey! She smiled. She knew that he had no intention of getting out by himself. It was pointless arguing with small children. They didn't understand it. She climbed up on the same stones Ascanius had used and stepped into the pond herself. The water felt cool and delicious against her legs.

'Elissa! Why are you in the water too?' Ascanius asked.

'I'm going to pick you up and take you to your father.'

'*No!*' Ascanius started shrieking.

'Shriek as loud as you like, silly boy. I'm still picking you up.'

She reached for him and he tried to wriggle out of her grasp, but Elissa was too quick for him and too strong. She lifted him, and hoisting him over her shoulder as though he were a bundle of washing, she walked to where Aeneas and Dido were standing and handed him into his father's arms. The boy was shouting so loudly that she only just caught Aeneas' words: 'What would I do without you, Elissa? Thank you, more than I can say. Will you come with me to take this naughty boy to his room? You know better than I do what must be done once we get there.'

'Yes, of course,' Elissa said. She had almost to run to keep up with Aeneas, whose long strides covered the distance between the garden and the palace in moments. As she reached the high, arched doorway to the central corridor, she turned to see that Dido herself was coming slowly up the path they had taken. The look in her eyes puzzled Elissa. She'd been laughing with them only moments before but now she looked worried. Was it worry? Or something else? She turned away and followed Aeneas to Ascanius' room.

'I can take him, sir,' she said. 'You don't have to bother with dressing him. I'll have to clean him up a little – the water in the pond is dirty.'

'He doesn't deserve you, Elissa,' Aeneas said, and handed the boy to her. He went to sit on the bed and watched as she took off Ascanius' wet clothes and led him to where a jug of clean water and a bowl stood ready.

'Stand still, Ascanius,' she said, wetting a soft cloth and beginning to wash him from head to toe.

'You're very good at that,' Aeneas said, and even though she couldn't see him, Elissa could tell he was smiling as he spoke.

'I've got a lot of younger brothers and sisters,' she answered. 'Not here, but in the village I came from.'

'How do you come to be working here?'

'I ran away from home. The queen's servants found me and . . . well, she was kind to me and took me in to work for her.'

'I'm very glad she did.'

'Is Ascanius here?' Anna had appeared at the door of the room. 'I've been told about your daring pond adventure, you funny boy,' she said, and went to embrace him. 'But it's time for your supper now, so come with me, little one, and we'll find you some delicious things to eat. Ready? Come along, now . . .'

She took Ascanius by the hand, smiled at Aeneas and bowed her head as they left the room together.

Elissa was alone with Aeneas. Should she say anything? What? She had no idea. Not only could she not speak, she seemed to have lost the power of movement as well. For the first time since she'd stepped into the pond, she became aware that her thin garments were soaking wet and clinging to her body. How could that be? The water had been shallow. When she stood in it, it reached no higher than her knees. But she'd bent down to pick up Ascanius and now . . . Was it possible that Aeneas could actually *see* her breasts? Her nipples? She picked up the linen towels that she'd used to dry the child and managed to hold them in such a way that they covered her. Aeneas got up from the bed and came over to where she stood.

'You're a lovely girl, Elissa. Has anyone told you that?'

'No,' she said. What was happening? Did these words mean anything, or were they just a polite remark?

He went on, 'They will, I promise.' Then he put one thumb under her chin and lifted her face. 'And whoever it is will be most fortunate.'

Should she thank him? Before she had time to arrange her thoughts into some kind of order, while she was still trembling with the complete unexpectedness of what Aeneas had just said and done, he leaned forward a little and kissed her on the mouth. Just one swift, soft touch of his lips on hers, and then he turned and walked away, and Elissa was left standing next to the window, feeling hot and cold at the same time, part of her wondering if she'd dreamed what had just happened. She went to sit on Ascanius' bed and didn't move for a long time.

Some time before dawn; the small bedchamber

'Oh Gods, yes,' Dido said. 'That *is* a day I remember. Or rather the night of that day.'

So she wasn't asleep after all. Elissa said: 'Can I get you something, lady? Some food? I know they're still awake in the kitchen, waiting to see whether you want something to eat.'

'To eat? No, nothing to eat. Thank you, Elissa. Shouldn't you be asleep? Although of course now you don't have to get up early in the morning for Ascanius. That should console you a little.'

'It doesn't though. I'd much rather feel tired and have Ascanius still here.'

Dido flung herself back on to the bed. 'And I, Elissa. And I. That night, after Ascanius fell into the fish pond – that was the first time Aeneas showed me his love. Told me of his feelings, I mean. It was then that I realized he could love me. I, of course, had made up my mind to marry him on his first night in Carthage, when I heard his stories and found myself enchanted by his voice, by him. I think it's possible, don't you? To be enchanted?'

'Yes, I do.' Elissa's mind was trying to grasp what Dido had just said. If Aeneas had kissed her that night ... What did it mean? *Perhaps* – this thought came to her like a bird flying into a room; and like a trapped bird bumping into windows and corners and desperate to find a way out, it whirled around in her mind – *he might have been thinking of me; of how he wanted to kiss me and maybe more than kiss me, even as he was kissing Dido for the first time.*

Elissa knew she was young and inexperienced, but since Aeneas came to Carthage, she had grown up very quickly. She smiled to herself. The queen was much older, but who was going to be the mother of Aeneas' child? Men (and she had known this for a long time: she had been observing them all her life and especially since starting to work at the palace) could be attracted to more than one person at a time. Very often love didn't come into it. Once, in the sewing room, one of the more vulgar of the sewing women had said: *For men, it's no more than a kind of itch. Anyone'll do to scratch it. They're not much different from dogs, when you come right down to it.*

'We had an argument that evening,' the queen continued. 'After the meal had been served. Iopas had sung some new songs and one of them was a love song that moved me deeply. When you're in love, Elissa, everything takes on an extra meaning. I can't remember how often I've listened to love songs and they've reached my ears and not my heart. But that night Iopas' words struck me and made me think.'

159

She reached for her lyre and began to pluck it again. 'Listen. I remember it. The whole song.

> '*Your eyes have made a flower bloom in my heart.*
> *Your voice has brought sweet music to my ears.*
> *Your mouth has spoken words that stir my blood.*
> *Your eyes are full of fire that lights my dreams.*
> *Your arms are empty. Take me in your arms*
> *and hold my beating heart close, close to yours.*
> *Kiss my red lips and waves of sweetest love*
> *will drown us both and cover us with bliss.*'

Dido's voice trembled. Tears flowed down her cheeks as she sang, and sobbing overcame her as she stumbled through the last line of the verse. Elissa said, 'It's a very pretty tune. I'm not sure about the words.'

Was that rude? Was she allowed to offer criticism of Iopas' verse? To her it always seemed to be too much, too florid, too worked on. She sometimes wondered whether Iopas really felt the things he wrote about, or whether he simply had a gift for finding words that would fit deep feelings if he did ever happen to have them. It seemed very strange to her that he could turn words this way and that and make them do whatever he wanted them to do when he was writing songs and yet not really know how to talk to a person when she was in front of him.

'The words *become* miraculous if they describe what you're feeling. That was what I wanted: for Aeneas to take me in his arms and crush me against him. I could

160

hardly eat. And we started a silly argument. About Troy and the war and whether the Greeks were justified in using a trick to get into the city, and I said that many things went on during wars which were wrong, but which you could perhaps justify because you wanted to win the battle, and this went on and on and trailed off into other things, and in the end I found myself begging him to stay in Carthage. Begging him not to leave me. What a fool I was!'

'No, lady, never a fool.'

'You're kind to me. And perhaps I will drink something, if you bring it to me.'

'With pleasure!' Elissa jumped up from the bed and went to the door. 'I'll fetch water.'

'And wine too. Some red wine with my water.'

'Of course.'

Elissa left the room and Dido lay down on the bed.

Anna

'You?' Dido said. 'I thought it was Elissa who was bringing me some water and wine.'

'I met her in the kitchen and took the jug and goblet from her. Here . . .' Anna decided to ignore the fact that her sister sounded irritated at this change. Dido would probably have been happier without me here, she told herself, but I don't care. She's my sister and I'm the one who should be looking after her. She said, 'Here, take a drink. The night is so hot.'

'Thank you. I didn't mean to sound— Oh, Anna, you know how I am. I can't sleep. I want to do nothing but think about him. Talk to someone about him. Remember words he said to me.'

Anna sat down beside her sister on the bed. 'I'm happy to talk to you about whatever you like. If that's Aeneas, then so be it. I'd rather not talk about him because I get angry all over again when I think of how he's just disappeared without so much as a word of thanks,

162

and after everything we did for him. *You* did for him.'

'D'you remember the night we discussed the war in Troy?' Dido said, and Anna looked at her helplessly. She's speaking as though I've said nothing. She hasn't heard a word I've said. She's in her own head, and if I want to communicate with her, I have to go into her head too.

She sighed and said: 'Yes, I remember. You were being obstinate. I was there, but couldn't hear exactly what you were talking about, of course.'

I'm lying, she thought. Never mind. I heard every word they said to one another that night.

Anna sat with a piece of embroidery on her lap, wondering how it was that Dido and Aeneas could be in a public room (in this case, the smaller room off the banqueting hall where the queen liked to eat when she was not entertaining visitors) and behave as though no one else was there with them. But I'm here, she thought as she stabbed a needle threaded with twisted silver into the dark cloth. She had suggested to Dido that perhaps the two of them, she and Aeneas, would like to be alone, but Dido wanted her to stay. Anna withdrew to a seat some distance away from them, and Dido then behaved as though she wasn't even in the room. She certainly doesn't notice, Anna reflected, that her sister is unhappy. Lovers are selfish, she thought. Why should she see? I've not spoken to her lately about my feelings for Iopas, and how my whole being is churned into misery and jealousy when I look at her and Aeneas and notice how happy they are. She sighed. It was unworthy to be jealous of her own beloved sister but she couldn't help it. She tried to imagine how she and Iopas would look, nuzzling into one another's necks, twining their fingers together and sipping from one another's lips as though they were bees seeking nourishment from the flowers.

'I can let you hear what they're saying,' said a voice in her ear. Anna sprang up, nearly dropping her embroidery. A woman with white hair piled up on top of her head and wearing a cloak edged with peacock feathers was standing beside her. 'Don't look so astonished. I'm Hera, wife to Zeus, and I'm anxious to foster this love between your sister and Aeneas. Can you see how they adore one another? Aphrodite and I have had to do very little to encourage it. The love has sprung up strongly, and almost spontaneously. Just listen.'

'I'm sitting too far away,' Anna murmured. 'And besides, they're whispering. It's hard to make out the words.'

'Take this,' said Hera, and handed Anna a small peacock feather, which glowed blue-green in the torch-light. 'Hold it and you'll be able to hear everything.'

'It's unseemly,' Anna objected. 'Lovers should be alone together.'

'Then throw the feather away,' said Hera, blending into the hangings on the wall until Anna could no longer see her.

She was on the point of doing exactly that, when curiosity overcame her. Perhaps it wouldn't be so wrong, she told herself. Dido is my sister. We're of the same blood. Also, no one will know. She put her embroidery down on the floor and held the feather tightly, surprised by how suddenly thrilling it was: to listen without anyone knowing you were listening. It was like being invisible: a little like being one of the Gods. Aeneas was speaking.

'You're stubborn as a mule,' he said, but he was smiling. 'You won't admit when you're wrong. And you *are* wrong about many things. Not least the war in Troy. I was there. I saw the results of that trick of Odysseus'.'

'A hero! That's what you are, Aeneas, and anyone who doesn't agree with you is naïve and ignorant.' Dido laughed. Anna could tell that her sister was more than a little drunk. Her head, she thought, is probably swimming as much as mine. She, Anna, had been with Dido and Aeneas for most of the day, and it had been full of small incidents that she had observed carefully. He'd held Dido's hand for a moment as we all walked in the garden, she thought. He twice put an arm out to guide her, once when we were near the temple and then again when they were approaching the harbour. And each time he touched her, Anna thought, I could imagine what she was feeling, even though it's a long time since anyone put his hands on me in such a way. I can remember how the blood begins to sparkle and ripple through the body.

'I've had enough of arguing,' Dido said. 'I'm more interested in persuading you to stay in Carthage, Aeneas. Stay with me, I beg you.'

As she spoke, Anna thought: What is she saying? She's a queen. How can she beg a man to stay as if she were just any woman? What's become of her dignity?

'Oh, my dearest Dido, how beautiful you are!'

Aeneas reached out then, and folded her into his arms. Anna nearly dropped the feather as she watched Dido trembling in every limb. Aeneas had pulled her close to him and his chin seemed to be resting on her hair. Her mouth was on the skin of his neck . . . Oh Gods, she *was* – she was putting out her tongue and licking the skin of his neck and pushing her chin up and moving her head so that she was higher, higher, and her mouth was on a level with his, and she fastened her lips on his like someone famished, dying of thirst, dying of longing.

'Dido!' He breathed her sister's name and his mouth pressed down and her lips opened and Anna heard her groan and saw her twisting in his arms as if she wanted to press herself entirely into his flesh.

When the kiss ended, Aeneas began to apologize, but Dido put her fingers on his lips and said: 'No, don't say a word. I wanted you to kiss me. You must know that I've been wanting it for a long time.'

'I didn't dare to think . . .'

Anna watched Dido pull away from him and sit up straight. She looked steadily at him, her mouth on the very edge of a smile. Her left hand was still holding his, the fingers intertwined.

'Does this mean you've changed your mind about setting sail for wherever it is you have to set sail for?'

Aeneas frowned and pulled his hand away. 'It's nothing to laugh about.'

'I wasn't laughing.'

'You were mocking me, Dido. Mocking what I told you of my destiny. I have to go – don't you understand? Hermes himself came to me in dreams. He was quite clear about what I had to do. About my duty.'

'I understand, I do, truly, but I also think you could be more . . . more distressed about it. Speak to your mother. Offer sacrifices to her and to Hermes. Tell them . . . Tell them how much you want to stay in Carthage with me. You do want to, don't you? Isn't it comfortable here? You surely have everything you want. If you are lacking anything, you only have to tell me and I will arrange for it to be brought to you, Aeneas.'

'You see?' Aeneas was smiling now. 'That proves you don't understand.'

He's looking at her as though she's his child, Anna thought. Indulgently.

Dido answered: 'I understand that you're proud and stubborn and the fact that I'm the ruler here is some-thing you can't quite get used to. Am I right?'

'Yes and no, Dido. Yes and no. *Of course* I understand that you're the queen. You rule the land well. You have power and you deserve it. I'm also grateful to you, as you know, for everything. But why don't *you* under-stand that being grateful is hard for me? It would be hard for any man, but particularly for one who has known for a long time that it's his destiny to found a great city across the sea from Carthage. We cannot escape our destiny.'

'But if you married me, Aeneas, I would share the throne with you. We could reign over Carthage together.'

Anna was so surprised that she almost sprang up at that moment. As though her sister would ever share power with anyone! That proves how far Dido has travelled from her normal self, she thought. What will he say? Will he agree to such a thing? No, he was shaking his head.

'I don't want to share power,' he said. 'And neither do you, Dido. For which I admire you. I could turn your offer upside down. Why do you not leave Carthage and come with me to found a new dynasty?'

'I would never do such a thing,' Dido answered. 'Why should I? Why is my kingdom somehow not as important as yours, Aeneas? Quite apart from the fact that Carthage is thriving and your future realm is nothing but a dream. I have subjects who rely on me for their welfare, their employment. Their livelihoods. And how do you know the Gods will do as they promised?'

'Because Aphrodite is my mother. She would never lie to me.'

For a while neither of them spoke. A silence had fallen between them and grew and grew until Anna wondered whether she ought to get up from her seat and say something to break it. Then Dido said, 'I'm going to my bedchamber now, Aeneas. I hope . . . I

168

hope that what I've said to you tonight will work on you as you sleep and change your mind. Remember that I've asked you to stay.'

'Kiss me once more before you go,' Aeneas said.

Dido was shaking her head. She seemed to Anna suddenly different, no longer feeling the effects of the wine, all at once a queen and not a woman in the throes of passion. 'No, Aeneas. I will not kiss you again till you agree to marry me. I have my pride. I don't want to be . . .' She hesitated. 'A pastime for you. A plaything.'

'Never, Dido. You would never be that. You know my feelings for you.'

'I thought I knew. Perhaps I was mistaken. We'll see. Tomorrow we go hunting in the mountains. The expedition has been planned for some days and we cannot postpone it without putting many people to great inconvenience. Will you be ready to leave at first light?'

'I will. And I thank you. We'll have good sport, I'm sure. Goodnight, dearest Dido.'

'Sleep well, Aeneas.'

She left the room, and a short while later, Anna followed her. She was so eager to reach her sister that she let the peacock feather drop to the floor. She bent down to pick it up again and it had vanished. That can't be, Anna thought. It was there, on the tiled floor, blue-green and glowing. Where could it have gone? I'll look for it tomorrow, she thought. Dido needs me now.

She reached her sister's room and saw the queen

lying face down on the enormous bed, beating her fists against the pillows.

'Anna? Is that you? Oh, Anna, will this night never end? I want the morning to come. I want . . . Oh, I'm mad with love for him. And he loves me. Did you see? Did you notice how he looked at me? How he kissed me? Oh, Gods, let this night pass quickly. I want to see him again. I want to be with him. Do you think I've lost my mind, Anna?'

'I think you're tired and have had too much wine. Go to sleep now.'

'Stay with me, Anna. Till I'm asleep. Like you used to do when we were girls.'

Dido fell asleep almost at once, but Anna sat at the end of her sister's bed for a long time, staring into the darkness, worrying about the future and offering silent prayers to both Aphrodite and Hera on her sister's behalf. She thought about Iopas. Much good her prayers were. Aphrodite and Hera hadn't listened to her pleas about Iopas. He wasn't interested in her and there seemed to be nothing she could do about it. There were times when he was kind. On one or two occasions he'd sat next to her at feasts, and once he'd recited to her some poems he'd written and she cherished the memory of how close together they'd been sitting then: on a pile of cushions in a sunny corner of the courtyard, with the palm trees making a latticework of fronds above their heads, and the air warm and caressing on their faces. I listened to them all, Anna thought, and I praised every one, but really I wasn't listening at all. I was relishing being so close to him. But at the end of the reading he went back to his chamber. He kissed my hand before he went, but oh, how much more I wanted from him! How much more I always want.

She stood up. I must leave Dido to sleep, she thought. I must go back to my own chamber. My lonely chamber. She walked through the darkened corridors of the palace and sent up yet another prayer to Aphrodite. Please, Goddess, let me not sleep alone for ever. Please, I implore you.

The next morning Anna came into Dido's room to help her dress.

'The white and silver,' Dido said. 'I want to be cool.'

'Hmm,' Anna said. 'Are you wearing a cloak over this dress? Or an overdress? You can see everything through this fabric, you know.'

'Perhaps. Yes, perhaps I will.'

It occurred to Anna that a cloak could easily be removed if Aeneas decided that was what he wanted.

'You'll come with us?' Dido asked. 'Please?'

'If you wish me to,' Anna answered. 'I'd be glad to escape the city for a while. Thank you. I will go and leave orders with the servants for what is to be done in our absence.'

'And put on your best clothes, dear sister. It will be a fine party!'

Almost dawn; the small bedchamber

Anna looked at Dido, who was sipping from the goblet of watered-down wine. The night would soon be over. Outside, the sky was almost black and she went to the window and gazed down at the city. Only a few lights showed there now, and the friendly yellowish glow cheered her. Down in the harbour there must be torches lit for the guards to see by, but she couldn't make out any movement yet on Aeneas' ships.

'You're longing for the daylight, aren't you?' Dido spoke, and Anna could hear that her voice was raw from too much weeping. 'You wish him gone. You wish this over, this night and my sorrow. You want it all to end.'

Anna turned to face her sister. 'And you want it to continue? You like being like this? Oh, Dido, think! Think how you were before he came and how you could be again. A queen, a ruler, powerful, beautiful, with everything to make you happy ... Can you not cease this crying and remember how it was before Aeneas came to the city?'

Dido looked up at her, and for a moment Anna hoped that there would be a light, a glimmer of understanding in her eyes. Let her come to her senses, she begged the unseen Gods on Olympus. Let her realize that the Queen of Carthage cannot continue to sit on a small bed in a narrow room with her knees drawn up under her chin, her eyes reddened with tears, her hair – the magnificent amber-coloured curls so carefully washed and tended and oiled and scented, the envy of every woman who saw her, the object of so many men's fantasies – knotted and tangled and unkempt. But no, she could see that her prayers had gone unheeded. Her sister's gaze was fixed on a spot above the door handle as though all the answers in the world were there, if only she could decipher them. Her lips were clamped together into a straight line and she brought the fingers of one hand up to her mouth and began to bite at the nails.

Anna shuddered and sat down on the bed, prepared to wait with Dido until the sky grew light again. Should she speak? Or should she simply pass the time by remembering? Dido's eyes were closed now, and Anna went back in her mind to the morning of the hunt. The morning of what her sister always referred to as her wedding day. Dido certainly put on her clothes that morning as though she were dressing for some special occasion. Usually, for the hunt, she wore a shift made of softest leather and boots that covered her legs almost to the knee, but on that day she put on her white and silver robes, almost as though she were choosing the garments that would come off most easily. Was she planning what would happen later and wanting it to happen? Surely not ... Dido had no powers to foretell the future, but perhaps Aphrodite was listening to her thoughts and preparing the ground for what was destined to happen that day.

Cubby

Daybreak approaching; the courtyard

What nobody ever told you about being a guard was, it was boring. Cubby was finding it harder and harder to stay awake. He'd tried all sorts of things to keep his eyes from closing. He'd walked round the bed, first in one direction and then in another. He'd sung himself some bits of songs he remembered, which weren't up to much because just as he was getting going, he forgot what came next. He went over things in his head, and sometimes something would happen which woke him up for a bit. There was the white dog and the silver lady or Goddess or whatever she was. Then Elissa went past on her way to the kitchen, but she didn't stop to talk. Then the queen's sister came by carrying a tray with a goblet and a jug of water on it, and that made Cubby feel very hungry and thirsty. Next time he saw someone, he'd ask them for something from the kitchen. One of the serving girls had brought him some food earlier on, but that was a long time ago. He

174

looked up at the sky above the courtyard and it was black all over. He'd already gone over in his head most of the things that made him happy: playing with Ascanius, being a friend to someone like Maron . . . But the trouble with thinking about stuff like that was you ended up with a sad story, because both Ascanius and Maron would be gone by the time the sun rose. Nothing there to cheer a person up.

He went to sit at the foot of the bed, and leaned against it. Something was stopping him. It felt like a long thin piece of wood. What was it? Cubby turned round and saw that he'd bumped his head on a bag which ought to have held some arrows . . . what did they call it? He didn't know the right word, but it was made of leather and there were no arrows in it now. He pulled it out and flung it higher up the pile of Aeneas' belongings and settled back against the bed. Arrows . . . Last time those were used was for the hunt. He'd only been on a hunt once in his life but that was enough. Cubby felt a bit strange whenever he thought about it, but he'd enjoyed it to begin with. Later on, it all got a bit weird.

Cubby couldn't get over being asked to go on a hunt with the royal party. It must have been Maron's doing, he thought, because the day before, Maron had come into the kitchen and spoken to Cook.

'It'll be hot up on the mountain, Cook, and I think you'll need help with menial tasks like putting fruit on trays,' he told him, and then winked at Cubby behind

Cook's back. Cook said nothing. He didn't speak very much at the best of times, and on this day he was busier than ever preparing fruit and bread and wine in leather bottles for the hunting party. Many baskets would be needed. Many water bottles, as well as those which held wine. And all day long, sides of meat would be lying in a bath of oil and herbs before they were threaded on to the spit and roasted in time for the feast, which would be prepared to greet the hunters when they returned to the palace. Maron was still talking to Cook.

'Cubby's the strongest boy you've got, I reckon. I think you should take him along with the others. He's good at fetching and carrying too. He'll be very useful.'

At last Cook had nodded his consent. He scowled at Cubby after Maron left the kitchen and said, 'Don't put a foot wrong, mind, or I'll send you back down to the palace before you can say roasted pig.'

'Thank you, Cook,' Cubby said, and made himself scarce.

The rest of the day passed slowly because he was so eager for the next morning to come, but in the end it was over. Cubby was up at daybreak, loading the horses with baskets full of food and utensils. And who'd have thought so many people were needed just so that Dido and Aeneas, the Lady Anna and some courtiers could go hunting? As well as the kitchen staff, Cubby walking proudly among them, there were guards on horseback, about twenty of them, and attendants, and Iopas was there as well. Perhaps after they'd eaten, Dido and Aeneas wanted someone to sing them songs. I'd much rather have a nap than listen to songs, Cubby thought as they trudged up to the hills. He counted eight horses loaded with wine and food and folded tents to put up when they got to a suitable spot. Maron was there, riding one of the horses, and he actually came and spoke to Cubby briefly before joining the others at the front of the procession.

'I'm looking forward to this, Cubby. Aren't you glad you came? They've seen some stag up here in the hills. It'll be a good day, right?'

Cubby opened his mouth to answer but Maron had already ridden off. I'd still be in the kitchen if it weren't for him, he thought. They reached a pleasant place after a bit, where there was room to put up the tents, and almost before Cubby had time to unpack the baskets he'd been put in charge of, men were rushing about with ropes, and shouting and heaving and puffing and blowing, and soon there was a kind of tent palace big enough for everyone in the royal party to sit down in comfortably, and another smaller tent a little way off for the servants and others to sit down in so that everyone could eat their fruit and cakes and drink their water and wine out of the glare of the sun. Cubby glanced into the royal tent and saw that cushions had been scattered around too. Grand people didn't like the idea of sitting on the hard ground either, so there were rugs in there as well. A horse had carried them up here on his back, all rolled up and tied to the saddle with leather thongs. Cubby had felt quite sorry for the poor creature.

The idea was that the hunting party would ride out after the stag for a bit and then come back and eat fruit and rest and drink, but then someone decided they'd better eat at least a bit first because the weather was turning funny.

'Storm coming,' said Cook, sounding sulky as he loaded grapes and figs and dates on to the trays they'd brought up with them. Cubby was standing ready to fetch and carry, and as soon as Cook gave him the signal, he took the food to the tent and came back for more. When he'd finished doing that, he began to look around for Maron, but couldn't see him any-where. He must be in the tent with the others, Cubby thought. Maybe talking to that Iopas. He sighed and sat down on a tree stump a little way off.

That storm will be here soon, he told himself. The clouds were huge and dark bluey grey, piled up like puffy mountains all over the sky. Occasionally a dart of lightning would shoot out of the clouds and the first one he saw made Cubby jump. I'm scared, he thought. I hate storms. The thunder sounded to him like a whole collection of barrels being rolled over a pave-ment, ready to crush him flat, and lightning, everyone knew, came from a powerful god called Poseidon, who brought death and destruction to those at sea who happened to annoy him. Cubby shivered and looked for somewhere to take shelter. He noticed something like the mouth of a cave a bit further up the path and went to explore it. As he walked towards the dark opening in the rock, he wondered what would happen if Cook needed him for something. Should he go back or go on? A flash of lightning decided him, and he made a dash for the cave just a few moments before the rain came washing down in torrents. The light had turned a funny colour too. It looked almost purple.

Cubby was just starting to explore the cave when he heard voices getting louder, which meant someone was coming. He hadn't reckoned on that happening. I daren't let anyone see me, he thought. They'll send me back to the tent, out into the storm. I can't go out there. The lightning will skewer me like a piece of meat and I'll roast alive. He ducked behind some rocks, and making himself as small as possible, squatted down with his arms around his knees.

'Come, Dido,' someone said, and Cubby recognized the voice of Maron's master, Aeneas. And he'd said *Dido*, which meant that she was here too. He nearly fell over in astonishment. What should he do now? If he made a dash for the opening of the cave, the royal couple would see him, and then what? Aeneas was still speaking. 'We'll go in here ... look. We'll be quite dry.'

'But what'll they say? The others?' That was the queen. Cubby peered through a gap in the rock and saw the two of them, the queen and Aeneas, both soaking wet. Their hair was dripping on to their shoulders and they were holding hands. The queen was wearing a dress made from thin material that was so wet it clung to her body and Cubby could see everything as clearly as if she'd been naked. He squeezed his eyes tight shut, wondering whether a terrible punishment awaited a kitchen boy who'd looked at the queen's . . . he didn't even like to say the word 'breasts' in his head. Didn't even like to think it, but he opened his eyes again and stared. He couldn't help himself.

'There,' Aeneas said. 'We're dry and safe and the storm will last for a while. There's no need for us to hurry.'

As he spoke, the Trojan was leading her further and further into the cave. Cubby could see, in the dim light that came in from the entrance, that it was huge, much larger than he'd thought at first.

'I think the Gods have visited this place,' the queen said. 'This is a kind of temple.'

'Aphrodite's here now,' Aeneas said, and the two of them stood still, facing one another in the middle of the cave.

'Where? I don't see her . . .'

'Here. On my lips. In my hands. Come to me, Dido. Let me kiss you.'

Cubby practically stopped breathing. He wasn't supposed to see stuff like this. Or hear such words either. In some way that he couldn't quite put his finger on, he knew that it was wrong to stare at the two of them, but his eyes were almost popping out of his head and his mouth hung open. Aeneas had his arms around the queen and was holding her so close that the whole of her body was squashed up against his. She didn't seem to mind that. Cubby saw her lift her face and kiss Aeneas and he tried to imagine what that would be like, and thinking about it made him feel most peculiar and he blushed and hid his eyes. Suddenly he could smell something delicious, like roses and almond blossom, and he sniffed as quietly as he could. Where did that perfume come from? He looked behind him and almost cried out. A beautiful woman had just appeared at his shoulder. How had she come in without him noticing? Who was she? Should he warn the queen and Aeneas?

'Sssh!' said the woman. 'Don't speak. I am Aphrodite, Goddess of Love, and that's all you need to know. My business is with Dido and Aeneas and the fact that you're here is completely unimportant. You will see things and hear things and that can't be helped. Fortunately, you'll forget most of it later. You're not the sort of person who keeps things in his memory, are you?'

Cubby shook his head. The Goddess said, 'Good. Now stand up, boy. You'll be more comfortable. They won't be able to see you. I've arranged matters so that they see and hear nothing but one another. Now I must leave you and speak to Dido.'

The Goddess drifted over to where Aeneas stood, still kissing the queen as though he never wanted to stop. Could a kiss go on for such a long time? Had it been a long time? Cubby couldn't tell. He had an idea that maybe he was dreaming and would wake up any moment now in his narrow bed down in Carthage, but no, there was the Goddess whose name he couldn't remember whispering to Dido, and he could hear every word: *He's my son. Take him, take him as your husband. Let him lead you to your marriage bed. Here, behind you, there's a hollow in the rock and I have lined it with soft leaves and wool from the youngest goats, and you can lie here and be together, and when you rise from this bed, you will be husband and wife. I have told you so. It's true and you want it, Dido. You want it more than anything . . .*

'I can hear her,' Dido was whispering right in Aeneas' ear, but Cubby could still hear every word. 'I can hear Aphrodite. She's speaking to me, Aeneas. She says we're man and wife . . . she says we're to be married.'

'She speaks nothing but the truth, for here is our wedding couch, see? Prepared by the Gods for us, Dido. How can you disbelieve?' He was laughing as he spoke, kissing her as he laughed.

Cubby watched as Aeneas picked up the queen and carried her over to the long hollow in the rock and laid her down on what looked like a cloud of white woolly stuff heaped up there.

'This is the softest bed . . .' she said to him, and he answered: 'Our bed.' Then he untied the queen's wet garments and Cubby practically stopped breathing. He was dimly aware of lightning flashing somewhere in the distance, but his whole attention was on the white limbs entangled on the couch right under his eyes, and he could hardly hear the thunder or the drumming of the rain outside the cave for the

182

moaning and cries that came from the two of them. Cubby knew what was going on. He'd heard talk in the kitchens about men and women and what they did together in the dark, and he thought his whole body was going to explode if he didn't stop looking and listening, and yet he couldn't stop. No one had told him how noisy it was, and the noises kept on and on, and then he saw the queen throw her head back and her long hair was trailing nearly to the ground, and then she cried out so loudly that the sound went right through him, and if he hadn't known better, he'd have thought someone was murdering her, and then Aeneas shouted out too, and Cubby wondered if the others could hear these noises from where they were in the tent, and he also wondered if the storm was loud enough to cover what was going on in here and thought maybe it was, and that was a relief.

'You'll forget most of this,' said the Goddess, whose name had already almost disappeared from his head. 'This is like a marriage and that's what Dido will tell everyone. It is a marriage that I have arranged and you can see how happy they are.'

'Yes,' said Cubby, but he was still staring at the queen and Aeneas, lying together naked with their legs and arms entwined. Then the queen turned over on to her back and there they were again – her . . . her *chest*, Cubby told himself. Her chest. He couldn't move. Would he ever be able to move again? Then Aeneas seemed to wake up and they started kissing, and Cubby looked around for Aphra-something but she'd gone.

The only way you could tell she'd been there was from the fragrance of roses and almond blossom that still hung in the air.

I'd better move before they get up, Cubby thought. He could see sunshine lying in a thick gold strip along the cave floor and there hadn't been any rain or thunder for a bit. He was safe to run away. Also, he thought they might be about to start up again. The queen was breathing heavily – he could hear her from where he was – and Aeneas was panting a bit too. Cubby didn't think he could deal with any more of that. Once was bad enough, he told himself. If they're going to go through the grunting and moaning and things again, I'm getting out now.

When he returned to the tents, Maron spoke to him and waved a hand. 'Where've you been, Cubby?'

He seemed happier than he usually was and that was because everyone had been drinking wine and water and eating everything while they waited for Aeneas and Dido to return to the tents. 'We were about to send out a search party for the queen and Aeneas and we'd have asked them to look for you too. But there they are on the path. They'll be here soon and then we'll have to move on, I suppose, and get down to the hunting. Shame really. I'm quite happy sitting here now that the storm's over. They must have taken shelter somewhere. You must as well, because you're quite dry. Here, have a drink. Take a fig or two. Bet you're starving.'

Maron patted the ground next to where he was

184

sitting and Cubby sat down gratefully. His head was still spinning with pictures of what he'd just witnessed, but as he drank the wine they faded a bit.

'Everyone!' Dido was there suddenly, at the entrance to the tent. 'Listen to me, please. I have something to announce.'

What if she says something about what happened in the cave? Cubby asked himself. He listened with the others as Dido went on: 'This is a great day. An auspicious day.' (What does that mean? Cubby wondered, but he couldn't ask, not while the queen was speaking.) 'Lord Aeneas, who was sent to Carthage by the favour of the Gods, has just become my husband. The Goddess Aphrodite had prepared a marriage for us blessed by Olympus and today is our wedding day. This hunt is no longer just a hunt but a celebration of our marriage, and there will be a feast in the palace tonight. But till then I'd like you all to raise a goblet in our honour and in honour of Aphrodite, who brought us together in our love.'

Cubby watched as everyone cheered and drank. A feast ... Well, he knew that, because he'd already helped Cook with the preparations before he left. Still, what with the feast being one to celebrate a marriage, they'd probably be asking for extra cakes or something. Extra work, that was certain.

'Aeneas married to Queen Dido, eh?' Maron was suddenly beside him. 'A bit surprising, I'd have thought. My master is supposed to be leaving Carthage. That's what he tells me, anyway, but I suppose Dido could come with us. Wherever it is we're going . . .'

Cubby shook his head. He didn't know much, but he did know that the queen loved Carthage. Surely she would never leave a place she'd had made for her specially? It was hers. He couldn't think about this because Maron was now talking to Iopas, who'd crept up on them in that quiet way he had. He must have been drinking a bit too, because he was chattier than usual.

'I'll be asked to compose a wedding ode,' he laughed. 'But what kind of wedding could it have been, with no one from the temple to perform it? What did our beloved queen mean by the Goddess Aphrodite blessing them? I don't see her anywhere.'

Then (later on, Cubby couldn't work out what made him speak) Cubby opened his mouth and said: 'I saw her.' That was enough. He wished he could swallow the words back into his stomach but that was impossible. What had he done? How could he go back and change matters? He couldn't. He blushed and hoped that Maron and Iopas might not have heard, but they had. Iopas was on him, quick as a snake on a mouse.

'Whatever do you mean? Where did you see her? And what did you see? How did you know it was a goddess?'

'In the cave. I saw her in the cave.'

'You were in the cave? With the queen and Aeneas?' Iopas' eyes were enormous. Cubby could tell he didn't really believe him. He nodded.

Then Maron chipped in and said, 'Tell us what you saw in the cave, Cubby.'

He spoke so gently that Cubby thought perhaps he wouldn't be in trouble if he did speak. He said, 'I didn't see . . . or rather, I can't remember very well. But there was a smell. A lovely smell, and a lady who said she was called Aphra-something.'

'Aphrodite,' Iopas cut in, impatient, and Maron waved his hand at him to make him shut up, for which Cubby was grateful.

'Yes. Her. She made them both lie down. That's it.'

'Lie down? Where?' Iopas again.

'Shut up, Iopas. Can't you see he's embarrassed? What, do you need drawings to tell you what went on? Use your head . . . They obviously got carried away, the two of them in that dark cave, and Dido thinks that it means they're married. That's it. That's all. Let's change the subject. Cubby's face looks as pink as a pomegranate . . . Don't worry, Cubby. You couldn't help being there. Have another bunch of grapes. Go on.'

Cubby took the fruit and ate it, glad that the interrogation was over. Iopas – he'd have gone on asking questions, you could see that, but thanks to Maron he'd got off without having to go into too much detail. As he ate, as he listened to the laughter and the merriment around him, with everyone in a good mood now that the sun was shining again and especially because of the marriage, what he'd seen in the cave began to blur in his head until it was no more than a dim memory. He tried to summon up what had happened, what he'd seen, but when he did, he came across a kind of wall in his head that prevented him from going back to that time. The Goddess had said he would forget, and it was true. Never mind, Cubby told himself. It was something interesting while it lasted.

Daybreak approaching; the courtyard

'You are wondering,' someone said, 'why you've been allowed to remember that day.'

Cubby sprang up and stood to attention. Here was someone he'd not seen before. Where were all these visitors coming from? He was no good as a guard and that was that.

'Nonsense, you're a perfectly good guard. There's nothing anyone can do to stop gods and goddesses from moving about. I am Hera, the queen of Olympus. Sit down again.'

'Yes, madam,' said Cubby, and peered at the person – the Goddess – who didn't seem to mind talking to him. He'd never before spoken to so many people in one night, but this was a very odd night indeed, and some of the chats had been with gods and goddesses, which was very peculiar. This one was white-haired and tall, and her cloak had peacock feathers all over it. He didn't know what to say to her, but she was talking again so that was all right.

'I've been sitting near you and remembering the day

of the hunt, and that is why you've been allowed to recall it too, for a while.' She sighed and for a moment seemed more like a mortal woman than a goddess. She said, 'Aphrodite and I fell out over that, you know. Marriage was never part of the plan. I knew that Aeneas had to leave and sail away from Carthage, and I suppose I let her get away with it because I saw no actual harm in it, but I was wrong. It wasn't a real marriage. That was Aphrodite misleading Dido, giving her permission to submit to her desires. That's all. But it's caused a great deal of unhappiness and that day was just the beginning. Never mind, what has to be has to be. You won't be troubled with these memories again, don't worry. I'll leave you now.'

She began to drift away in the direction of the kitchens. Cubby closed his eyes. This night was also turning out to be longer than any other night he'd ever lived through.

Iopas

Before dawn; the palace kitchen

The night, which had lasted far too long already in his opinion, wasn't showing any sign of turning into morning. Iopas was sitting at a table in the kitchen which Cook used for preparing food during the day. It was clean and well-scrubbed but you could see the thousands of marks left by knives chopping vegetables or fruit or even meat over many moons. He'd been hungry, and had come down to find a piece of bread or some grapes, and besides, he was sick of the sight of his own room, which seemed to him full of nothing but half-finished poems and anxious thoughts. He'd counted on being alone, but when he came into the kitchen and found Elissa sitting on one of the benches at the kitchen table, he was happier than he'd been for a long time. Elissa! But she wasn't alone, and within a moment of registering her presence, he saw that her friend Nezral was sitting beside her. It was all he could do not to swear out loud. What better opportunity

190

would he ever have of getting Elissa on her own in the middle of the night? And here was her friend, spoiling things.

'Iopas!' Nezral said. Her fairish hair fell to her shoulders and her nose looked sharper than ever. She reminded Iopas of a skinny bird. 'Welcome. Are you hungry too? We couldn't sleep. Well, I could, but Elissa couldn't, and I woke up just as she was leaving our room. It's been a long night, hasn't it?'

'It has. And yes, I was hungry. And I can't sleep either, for worrying about our queen.'

'The Lady Anna has taken her some wine and water,' said Nezral. 'And some fruit too, I think. Which is good. They say she hasn't touched a morsel since last night.'

Iopas wished Elissa would say something. He'd been feeling a small stirring of hope that perhaps things would be different in Carthage now that Aeneas was leaving. Elissa might be upset at first but that would pass in the end and then maybe he could find a way round the problem of declaring his love. He'd already decided that if everything went well, he'd talk properly to Anna and make up some story about his imaginary betrothed in the city and how she'd fallen in love with someone else. Gods, love was complicated! But he'd work it out somehow. It would have helped a lot if he'd found Elissa by herself.

'Poor Dido!' said Nezral. 'I feel so sad for her. They say she hasn't even combed her hair since she woke up.'

'You'd have to have a heart of stone to look at Dido now and not feel a great sorrow,' he agreed, glancing at Elissa, who still hadn't said a word. She was staring down at her hands and her face was greeny-white, the colour of some cheeses. Her eyes were red-rimmed from too much crying. He went on: 'I blame Aeneas. How could he treat a great queen in such a way? As though she were any common woman?'

Iopas was clear-sighted enough to realize that his anger was partly a kind of envy. Ever since the Trojan came to Carthage, there wasn't a woman to be found who didn't start swooning every time you mentioned his name. It had become tiresome after a bit and Iopas, who at first had admired the man (and you couldn't deny he had a sure-fire story to tell about the war in Troy – Iopas smiled at his own wit: *sure-fire* story . . . the war in Troy), ended up a little irritated by everything to do with him. Anyway, there Aeneas was, and suddenly no one had eyes for anyone else. Aeneas, on the other hand, had eyes only for Dido. Or at least that was what Iopas thought for a long time, and then he started noticing how much time the Trojan was spending with his child. From that observation a thought sprang up: Would he be spending so many hours in the nursery if the nursemaid wasn't so pretty?

The jealousy he felt became worse than ever. Iopas started to see things. Aeneas looking at Elissa. Elissa looking at Aeneas with such undisguised adoration that it was quite embarrassing sometimes. Once or twice in the last couple of months he'd seen Aeneas sliding out of deep shadows among the colonnades around the courtyard, and lo and behold, a few moments later, there Elissa would be. Had she been hiding there all along? Had they been snatching a kiss in the dimness during those hours when the sun was at its height? Dido often retired to her bedchamber for a rest after the midday meal when the heat was stifling, and Iopas had observed that during the last few moons she'd started going to her chamber alone. He found himself thinking about Elissa and Aeneas and Dido far too often, and they hadn't been pleasant thoughts.

Elissa stood up from the table in one swift movement and ran out of the room without saying anything. Iopas jumped up to go after her but Nezral put a hand on his arm and said, 'Let her go. She's on her way to the privy, I think. She goes there a lot . . . She's feeling – well, not herself, shall we say?'

'What do you mean, Nezral? Why isn't she herself?'

'I can't tell you, Iopas. She'd kill me. She made me promise not to say a single word and I can't. I really, really can't.'

Nezral was a sharp-nosed girl who wasn't exactly attractive but was clearly clever and moreover had her ear to the ground as far as gossip among the servants was concerned. What to do now? If he bullied her, she'd clam up. And what if Elissa came back and found their heads together? He decided to use flattery and gentleness and see what that might lead to. He slid along the bench a little closer to the girl.

'You don't have to tell me anything,' he said. 'I can see Elissa is sad. She was so fond of Ascanius.'

'You have to be joking!' Nezral laughed. 'Well, she does love the boy, of course she does, but it's not him she's pining for. It's his father.'

'Everyone knows that Aeneas and Dido were man and wife,' said Iopas. 'How does she come to pine for him? Perhaps she's only crying for Dido's sake. She loves the queen like a mother.'

Nezral glanced over her shoulder towards the door, to make sure that no one was approaching. She turned her body towards Iopas and lowered her voice to a whisper.

'What they say is: Aeneas and the queen are no more married than you and I, Iopas. They say that during the hunt – you remember that day – the two of them went into a cave and . . .' She blushed and lowered her head. 'I don't want to say but you know what I mean . . . And then when they came out, Dido told everyone they were married. Just like that.'

Iopas said nothing. That was exactly the thought he'd had on the day of the hunt: that this was no proper marriage but only two people who'd got a little carried away, what with the storm and the wine and, apparently, the presence of a goddess. He'd been sceptical about the goddess bit, but then later on he found that the inhabitants of Olympus did indeed make themselves known to mortals. He said: 'But what has this to do with Elissa?'

'I can't say. She made me swear I wouldn't utter a

word. Let's just say that she has the very best of reasons to wish him still here.'

'Are you saying she loved him?' Iopas braced himself for the answer.

'Yes, of course,' Nezral said. 'She thought she was keeping it such a big secret, but we all knew. Or guessed. I did, anyway. Didn't you?'

'Perhaps,' Iopas murmured. 'Yes, I did.'

'But there's more,' Nezral whispered. 'She'd kill me if I said a word, but there's much, much more.'

At that moment Elissa came back into the room, her face still white but with less of a greenish tinge and the front of her dress damp. She must have been washing her face, Iopas thought.

'Come, sit here, Elissa. I'll fetch you some water. And something to eat. Bread . . .' Iopas stood up and went to the shelf where bread left over from the day was kept. He picked up a long flat loaf and brought it to the table, together with some cheese and fruit and a bowl into which he poured some olive oil from a jug standing on the wide sill of the window. 'You should eat,' he said.

'Thank you, Iopas,' she said, and he stared at her as she ate, grateful that at last she was speaking to him. He scarcely noticed Nezral leaving the room.

Elissa had been a child when she first came to the palace, but no longer. She had long dark hair that fell to her shoulders, golden olive skin (when she wasn't feeling tired and upset) and dark eyes that were almost purple in certain lights. *Eyes like plums* didn't work as poetry, which was a shame. In those days Elissa was slim and boyish, with no breasts to speak of. Her figure was very different from Dido's, whose bosom was the envy of women and an object of lust for most of the male population of Carthage. Aeneas tiring of one body shape and wanting to try another – could matters be that simple? Well, even if that was all it had been, he was heartily glad to see the back of the Trojan. Iopas watched Elissa as she sat in front of him. Was he imagining it, or were her breasts larger than they used to be? He didn't know very much about the size of young women's breasts in general, but on the subject of Elissa he was something of an expert and he had looked at her more carefully than he'd ever looked at any other person. He'd always thought of her as having very small breasts, but these looked . . . they were straining against the fabric of her robe. She seemed, in fact, altogether plumper than usual. Had she been eating in secret? Not wanting to interrupt her while she ate, Iopas let his thoughts go back to the night when he realized that the love between Aeneas and the queen was doomed.

Iopas had made it his business to chart the progress of Dido's love affair with the Trojan and it seemed to him that if the hunting party was the proper beginning, then a year and more had already passed since that day. Now he was of the opinion that during the last three moons Aeneas' interest in Dido had begun to wane. Iopas noticed that the Trojan was spending less and less time with the queen. And when they were together, Iopas often overheard him talking of leaving one day and not staying in Carthage, and how his destiny was to sail away, until you could see that Dido had become heartily sick of hearing about it. She'd almost stopped begging him to stay. Sometimes she simply walked out of the room when the subject arose. You could tell he was restless.

One night, after a feast, Iopas had been on his way back to his chamber when he noticed that the queen and Aeneas were still in the courtyard, sitting on the stone bench he often liked to sit on when the shade made it a cool spot. He could see the two of them together in the bright moonlight that fell through the leaves of the palm trees. The trees were planted in huge round pots, and now it appeared to Iopas that the flowing lines of the patterns painted on them had become real snakes and dragons writhing over their curved sides. Annoyingly, from where he was standing he couldn't catch what the queen and the Trojan were saying to one another and he was about to move away when someone spoke in his ear. He nearly fainted from the shock. A woman, tall and well-built, with white hair piled high on her head and wearing a cloak edged with peacock feathers, was standing at his shoulder. 'I fear that there is trouble between those two,' said this person. 'Listen . . .' and she put a peacock feather into his hand.

Iopas took it and had the presence of mind to say: 'Thank you . . . but who are you?'

'Hera, wife to Zeus and friend to Aeneas and the

queen of Carthage. This love is doomed, you know.'

Iopas found himself nodding. Hera continued, 'You'll know when you've heard them speak. Keep hold of the feather.'

He opened his mouth to thank her again but she had gone. Perhaps I imagined it, he thought, but then where did this feather come from? He held it, and suddenly became aware that he could catch what the couple on the stone bench were saying to one another, even though they were speaking in low voices and were sitting far away on the other side of the courtyard. He held the feather a little in front of him and raised it in the air, and as if it was catching the words and bringing them to his ear, he could now hear them even more clearly. It was as though he were sitting beside them. Aeneas began to nuzzle Dido's neck. Iopas saw the queen relaxing, and she turned and kissed her lover on the lips. 'This is the best time, Aeneas,' she murmured. 'For a baby. The wise woman says so – the moon is full. We'll have a baby . . . the next King of Carthage . . .'

Aeneas pulled away from her. You'd have thought a bee had stung him. 'What are you talking about? What baby? I don't want a baby. Who told you I wanted children? I have my son and he's enough for me. How can I have a baby with you?'

'Why are you so angry? You've never spoken to me like that before.'

'You've never tried to trick me into making you pregnant before.'

'How can you say that? It's not a trick. Cast your mind back, Aeneas. Didn't it occur to you that all our lovemaking might produce children? Isn't that what marriage is for?'

'Zeus and Hera and all the Gods, give me patience! For the last time, Dido, I'm *not* married to you! I'm not married to anyone. We got a bit carried away in the cave, I grant you, but marriage? It's completely ridiculous. You're crazed.'

'Your own mother sanctioned it. She was there, I tell you. I saw her. She told me.'

'I've heard this from you many times, Dido. It's madness. What you saw was a kind of dream. We were . . . You've forgotten how we were.'

'How do you dare to call me mad? What about the bed? Prepared and lined with wool and fragrant leaves – that was her work.'

Aeneas laughed. 'You're naïve, beloved. That hollow – probably been used by shepherds and passers-by for generations. Could even be a well-known feature of the area – the place everyone goes when they want to be alone. How could it possibly have been Aphrodite? Don't you think she would have managed a little more luxury for us?'

'We didn't need luxury, Aeneas. You're the one who's forgotten what it was like, up in that cave. Suddenly what happened there means nothing to you.'

'It does *not* mean nothing! It means what it *was*. *Really* was. You're enough to drive a man crazy with

199

your fantasies. What it meant was I wanted to make love to you. And that's what we did. We made love. End of story.'

'Oh, no. Not the end of the story at all. Who are you to decide where it ends? It's my story as well, and part of that is children. I want an heir to take over my kingdom when I die.'

'Not from me, though. I don't need that complication. My life's difficult enough as it is.'

Iopas had to hold the feather away from him. He hardly needed it any longer because Dido began to shout, shrieking at Aeneas like any common fishwife. Anyone who happened to be awake would have heard her from the other side of the palace.

'Difficult? How can you say that? I've done everything for you. Saved you from a miserable death on the sea and given you shelter and protection. Built you ships and let your men live in my city and bestowed on you all the riches at my command, to say nothing of my love. You're an ungrateful bastard and I don't care if I never see you again. Go. Go and don't come back. I hate you, Aeneas, and I must be mad, as mad as you say, to have fallen in love with you in the first place.'

The queen stood up then and ran away to her bedroom. Iopas wondered whether he should stay there and see what Aeneas did, or whether he should follow the queen. In the end he did neither. He went to his bedchamber and took the peacock feather with him. He distinctly recalled putting it on his writing table before he sank onto his bed, but in the morning, when he woke up, it had vanished.

From that time onwards, he'd started to notice that Aeneas was paying less and less attention to Dido and spending more and more time with Elissa.

Before dawn; the palace kitchen

Iopas looked at Elissa. She had finished eating the bread and was now resting her head on her folded arms. She sat up quickly – she must have felt his gaze on her – and turned to face him.

'Don't stop sleeping, Elissa,' Iopas said. 'You must be as tired as everyone else. I don't think anyone's resting quietly in their beds tonight, are they?'

To his astonishment, Elissa's reaction to this was to burst into tears. Iopas was used to crying women. Anna often wept, for no good reason that Iopas could make out, and he always knew the soothing words to say. The great secret was not to ask questions, just to murmur and reassure. He wondered whether he dared, and then decided that there was nothing to be lost. He placed one arm around her trembling shoulders. He said, 'There now, Elissa, please don't cry. It's a sad night, to be sure, but crying won't help Dido. She needs those of us who love her to be strong.'

'I know,' Elissa wailed. 'I know, and that makes it harder for me. Oh, Iopas, I'm so miserable.'

Iopas had to stop himself saying something along

the lines of: *Tell me something I don't know,* and said instead: 'Tell me what's worrying you. It may help you to talk about what's making you unhappy.'

He wasn't convinced of the truth of this last remark, but people said it constantly and perhaps it was true. Elissa sniffed and sat up and wiped some tears off her cheeks.

'He's gone, Iopas. Aeneas has gone and I can't tell anyone how I feel about that, because we're supposed to be feeling for Dido and she was his wife and I am . . . I'm nothing. Nothing but his son's nursemaid.'

'Well . . .' Iopas wanted above all for Elissa not to stop speaking. He knew that once you got them started, young girls were apt to tell you all sorts of stuff they didn't mean to let out in the first place. They got carried away with the sound of their own words and secrets poured out of them. He said now: 'Some people think that our queen wasn't truly married to Aeneas. Not in the way most people get married.'

'But the cave . . .'

'That's the story Dido told us on the hunt. You weren't there, Elissa. You were in the palace with Ascanius, but this is what happened. A storm blew up and Dido and Aeneas disappeared into a cave. None of us noticed it, but they must have done. Dido came out a few hours later, by which time we were pretty fed up, and announced that they were married. That Aphrodite herself had married them. Well, you know what that means, don't you?'

Elissa's eyes were wide, so Iopas continued. 'It means

202

that the cave . . . That was where they first . . . Where they . . . You can guess what they did in there, can't you?'

Elissa burst into a new storm of tears. 'I can't bear it. I don't even like to think about the two of them together. It's – it's like a torture to me!'

'But why, Elissa? Married or not, they've been sharing a bed for more than a year.'

'But he didn't really want to,' Elissa whispered. 'That's what he told me. She put a spell on him. He told me that as well.'

Iopas felt as though the breath had been knocked out of his body. Aeneas under Dido's spell? Reluctant to share her bed? What nonsense was this? The girl had clearly taken leave of her senses. He searched around for words that would encourage rather than stem the flow of Elissa's confessions.

'When did he say such things, Elissa?'

'Do you promise to tell no one, Iopas? I can't say anything unless you swear.'

He nodded, and that seemed to be enough for Elissa. I haven't sworn, Iopas told himself, I haven't said a word and she hasn't even noticed. She *wants* to speak. He put out a hand and touched her gently on the arm. He took a piece of bread she hadn't eaten and began to nibble at it. It occurred to him that he was more likely to find things out if some of his attention was not on Elissa.

She continued: 'He told me when we were together, alone. It's been happening more and more lately.

Since the winter he's been coming to see Ascanius. He used to come and kiss him goodnight, but in the last few moons he started spending some of the afternoons with his son. And talking to me. That was when he told me that he was going to have to leave Carthage. I asked him how he'd feel about saying goodbye to the queen and he *did* say it would make him sad, but then he said' – Elissa looked down at her fingers intertwined on the table in front of her – 'he said he'd miss me too. He told me I was beautiful and that it was a pleasure to be with me and not have to listen to constant complaints and demands and the queen begging him to stay. He said . . . he said I was restful. And then one night he stayed with me till morning.'

'Did he . . .' How am I going to say this? Iopas wondered. He swallowed the bread and continued, 'Did he force you to do anything . . . ?'

'Oh, no! I'm not sorry for what I did. I don't regret anything. I wish that night could have gone on for ever. You can't imagine what he said to me, Iopas – such things . . .'

Iopas was suddenly cold in spite of the heat of the night. He'd asked and now he was getting an answer, and listening to Elissa's outpourings was hurting him. There was a pain deep under his ribs, as though someone had come at him with a knife. He could scarcely breathe. He wasn't used to such feelings, which were there because he *could* imagine, better than Elissa knew, exactly the words, and worse than that, exactly the sounds and the movements and then the unguarded noises and the way limbs entwined and twisted and writhed. He could see the two of them – Aeneas and this young girl – and he noticed that his hands had clenched themselves into fists without him being aware of it. He closed his eyes. Should he stop her speaking? Could he bear to hear more? Wasn't this enough? It was – but he had to know if what he had begun to suspect was true.

'Elissa, may I ask you something?'

'Yes, I'll tell you everything. There's no point in hiding anything now.'

Iopas went on, 'Are you carrying Aeneas' child? Are you pregnant?'

She didn't answer, but nodded and then covered her face with her hands. He could hear from the way she was breathing that the tears were coming again. Iopas was filled with unaccustomed emotions. He was used to dealing with desire and with his growing love for Elissa, but these feelings were mingled with anger at Aeneas, disgust when he imagined – and how could he not? – the two of them together, and an unworthy voice in his ear saying: *She'll have less excuse to refuse me now. She's no longer a maiden. She lay with Aeneas. Why shouldn't she also lie with me? I'm her friend. I could look after her. I must try . . .*

He said nothing, but put his arm around Elissa's shoulders and hugged her to him. At first she didn't resist and seemed pleased to be comforted. But then he turned her face to his and started to kiss her and touch her breasts, and her reaction took him so much by surprise that he nearly fell off the bench they were sitting on.

'*No!*' she screamed, standing up. 'How could you, Iopas? I thought you were my friend and I've told you my deepest secret, and now here you are, trying to kiss me and . . . I don't know what made you think you could do that. Have I ever shown you that I'm interested in you in that way? Ever? By so much as a glance? You're taking advantage of my position. You know I'm sad. You know I'm pregnant, so of course it follows that I'll just go with anyone who happens to want me. Well, I'm sorry, Iopas, but I'm not interested. I won't ever be, so don't think I will. I'm going to bed now.'

She ran out of the room without looking back and Iopas was left staring at the plate in front of him. At first he was simply offended. What right did she have to refuse him? He wasn't as big and strong and handsome as Aeneas, that was true, but there was nothing wrong with him. Didn't Anna, who was the queen's sister after all, almost throw herself at him whenever she got the chance? If he was good enough for the queen's sister to love, then surely Elissa . . . She'd insulted him. His manhood. His looks. Everything about him. She'd practically said he wasn't good enough for her.

He tore off a piece of bread and stuffed it into his mouth. He was, he acknowledged, hurt by her refusal, but as well as that he found himself almost trembling with rage. Fury. He couldn't remember feeling as angry as this ever in his life. He began to see what he was going to do. If Elissa thought she could get away with treating him like dirt – Gods, the ingratitude of the girl! He'd befriended her; he'd offered to help her. What was the matter with her? – she was very much mistaken. He knew how to punish her. A plan was blossoming in him in exactly the same way as a poem did: starting out from a tiny seed of an idea and putting out branches and leaves and acquiring weight and substance and a shape. Yes, *that* was what he had to do next. He left the kitchen and made his way to Dido's small chamber. The door was standing open and he looked in.

'Is that you, Iopas?' Dido sounded as though she had just woken from a sleep. 'You can come in. I sent Anna away. She insists on trying to console me. I can't bear it. What have you got to tell me? I can see that it's something. Speak to me.'

Iopas sat on the floor next to Dido's bed and began to speak. Softly, word after word came from his mouth and wound itself into a story. Dido listened. She might be marble, Iopas thought, looking at her as she lay completely still on the narrow bed. When he finished speaking, silence hummed and swelled in the room, and Dido lay there, saying nothing for a long time.

When she spoke at last, she said: 'You may go, Iopas. I don't want to see or speak to anyone.'

More people, Iopas thought, ought to wake up before it was properly light and enjoy the beauty of the violet shadows and the dove-grey glow that filled the corridors and made the dark corners of the palace look mysterious and strange. The silence was soothing too, and as he walked towards the maidservants' quarters in search of Elissa, he turned over in his mind the first lines of a poem about dawn and the dark time that came just before the light burst from behind the mountains to the east. He almost jumped out of his skin when someone spoke his name in a whisper.

'Iopas? It's me . . . Anna.'

'You startled me,' he said. She was sitting on one of the stone benches set into the recesses that lined the main corridor. 'What are you doing here before daybreak?'

Aware that he'd spoken sharply, more from shock than anything else, he added more gently: 'I'm sorry . . . I didn't think anyone else would be awake.'

'Who can sleep on such a night? I'm sick with worry and can't rest. Will you sit beside me for a moment? It would comfort me, Iopas.'

He sat down and sighed. I don't need this, he thought. It's too late. I'm exhausted. He looked at her, with her straight brown hair hanging down on either side of her pale face. Dark half-circles under her eyes looked like bruises. Her thin lips were almost colourless. Her clothes, in which she took such pride, were creased and looked as though she'd been wearing them too long, and her perfumed oil, which reminded Iopas of jasmine flowers when he was feeling particularly kind, tonight called to mind something not quite fresh – dead flowers, perhaps. Maybe that was a poem too. She said, 'Where have you come from?'

'I've been with the queen. I had something to tell her. And' – this occurred to him all at once as a good excuse for leaving Anna quickly – 'I have to speak to Elissa at once so I can't sit here, I'm afraid.'

Anna put a hand on his arm. 'Just for a moment longer. Oh, Iopas . . .'

Iopas could feel anger flaring within him. How could he be rid of this woman who loved him too much and whose love he couldn't return? If she'd been almost anyone else, he'd not have hesitated this long. He'd have been brutal right from the beginning. Told the truth: *I can't love you. I couldn't ever love you. Go away. Leave me alone.* Perhaps in those very words. But Anna was the queen's sister, and because he wanted to remain at the palace as the court poet, he had to put up with this cloying attention. He said suddenly, 'I've just told your sister something. It's not generally known but I felt I had to say something to Dido.'

'Can't you tell me, my dearest one?'

Iopas thought: *My dearest one . . . Oh, Gods,* and sat up straighter and moved slightly away from Anna on the stone bench. He said, 'I don't really think . . .'

Anna looked so downhearted that for a moment Iopas felt quite sorry for her. Then an idea came to him and he couldn't stop himself. He didn't know exactly why what he planned to do was such a pleasant prospect but suddenly he felt powerful: like a kind of god who could take someone and change their life

209

and their fate for ever. He said: 'I told her that Elissa's pregnant.'

Anna swayed slightly, bending forward over her knees and making small sounds like an animal in pain, hiding her mouth with her hand. Iopas was ready for her to faint or vomit, but she collected herself and said: 'Are you sure?'

'Quite sure. I have to go and find Elissa now, Anna. I'm sorry.'

'Wait! Wait!' Anna cried. 'Tell me who the father is, Iopas, I beg of you.'

Iopas smiled. 'Oh, I can't tell you that, Anna. I gave my word to Elissa.'

'Does my sister know?'

'I can't tell you more, Anna. I have to go. Now.'

'I can guess, Iopas. Everyone in the palace can see that you're devoted to Elissa. Who else could it possibly be? Who else does she see all the time? Oh, Iopas, I beg you . . . Don't lie to me. I can see it on your face. It's dark but I can tell you're blushing. It's *you*, isn't it? You're the father of Elissa's baby . . . Oh Gods! Tell me, Iopas. Please.'

Iopas stood up. Anna clung to one of his arms and wouldn't let go.

'Leave me alone, please, lady. I have to go,' he said, and he pulled his arm away and left her. He was aware of a peculiar feeling in his stomach. It wasn't unpleasant. He had hurt Anna. She loved him and now he could feel her behind him, burning with anguish, furious with him and sick with jealousy of Elissa. He had done all that and he couldn't feel regret, only a thrill that he had the power to arouse such feelings in someone. Well, he couldn't help it if she'd come to the wrong conclusions about everything. Anyway, he told himself, she'll find out who the real father is as soon as she goes to see her sister. Till then, let her suffer a little. He imagined Anna weeping, wiping her red eyes, going to Dido and moaning. Her misery will end then, he said to himself, but Elissa made me suffer and that isn't going to stop. Why shouldn't Anna know what that feels like? Learn how painful love can be. He smiled. There was no end to the poems he could write about that!

Elissa

Before dawn; the courtyard/the palace gardens

If I don't get out of this palace, Elissa thought, I will
faint. I'll fall over and be sick and not be able to get up.
I need the air, the sky, the stars. She could feel the walls
beginning to close in and loom over her, and she ran
through the corridors with tears in her eyes, hot with
fury after what Iopas had said to her. Had tried to do
to her. She wrinkled her face up with disgust as she
remembered the taste of his lips on hers, however brief
the contact had been. Not only was she raging at his
suggestion (what had she ever done or said to him that
made him think she was keen to be his beloved?
Nothing); she was also sad to think that now, because
of his stupid behaviour, even the politeness they'd
shown to one another would be almost impossible for
her. How could she ever see his face again without
wanting to hit him? And as for what she had told him:
could she trust him to keep her secret? Everyone knew
what a gossip he was. No, she'd made him swear. Surely

he wouldn't break such an oath? I can't worry about that now, she told herself. It's hard enough to stop myself weeping all the time.

Elissa had reached the courtyard, and she could see, from looking at the sky, that the night was almost over. I'll go into the garden and no one will be there, she thought. I can wander wherever I like and no one will know. She had it in her mind to visit the fish pond and sit on the bench where she used to sit so often when she was looking after Ascanius. In the last few days Aeneas had come and sat there with her quite often. There were always guards and other servants walking about, so they could never embrace or refer in any way to what had passed between them, but still, it pleased her to have him near her. She sometimes contrived to brush her arm against his, to lean on him a little for a brief moment, and when that happened, she found it hard to breathe normally.

Cubby was sitting by the bed, still on guard. Elissa went over to talk to him. It must be so boring, just being there on his own the whole night long. She felt sorry for him. She smiled at him, even though she felt far from cheerful. I can't seem any different, she thought. I can't let him guess how miserable I am.

'Aren't you bored, Cubby? It's a long time to stay in one place.'

'Hello, Elissa. I don't stay in one place. I walk about. This bed is so big that if I don't watch out, someone could sneak up and pinch something from the other side. The side I'm not on, I mean. Why are you

213

walking about? I thought you'd gone to bed long ago.'

'I did. But I couldn't sleep. And now I'm going for a walk in the garden.'

'A walk? It's night time still. No one goes for a walk at night. That's silly.'

'Well, I don't see why they can't, do you? There aren't *rules* for walks.'

Cubby looked puzzled. 'Are you sure there aren't rules?'

'Quite sure. Stop worrying. Everyone's busy with the queen. No one's going to care what I do.'

'If you say so,' said Cubby, and stood up. 'And I think the night'll be over soon. See, the sky's a bit pale over there.' He pointed upwards.

'Yes, it'll soon be morning. I'll be glad when it is. And I'm sure you will be too.'

Cubby traced a pattern with the toe of his sandal on the dusty stones of the courtyard. 'Not really. I like it here.'

Elissa felt embarrassed. Of course he wouldn't want to go back to the horrible work he must have to do in the kitchens. She said, 'Maybe you can be a guard again. Sometime.'

Cubby nodded and said nothing. He obviously couldn't imagine another situation where such an opportunity might arise, and if Elissa was honest, neither could she, but she'd felt obliged to say something encouraging.

The guards at the main doorway nodded as she came out of the palace. She was ready with a story if they'd wanted one, but they recognized her and probably thought that she was on some errand or other – though what would someone be doing just before dawn in the deserted garden? The truth was, they were most likely exhausted with standing guard through the night and thinking only of their beds.

Elissa made her way to the bench. The dim light changed everything, and trees that were simply tall and graceful in the daylight became menacing. Shadows spread around everything, strange shapes that changed and shifted as you looked at them. The pond was a flat silver disc: a full moon trapped in a marble bowl, and every now and then some bubbles breaking at the surface indicated the presence of the fish. Odysseus – where was he? Tears came to her eyes when she remembered Ascanius' grin as he sat in the water, holding the fish in his little hands.

She sat down on the stone bench. One of the reasons she'd chosen to come here was because it had a good view of the harbour. I can sit here without moving, she thought, till dawn. Till the tide turns and he leaves. I can watch him sailing away. She didn't yet know whether she could bear to do that, but in any case Elissa was quite determined to keep away from Iopas and as many other inhabitants of the palace as she could. She wanted to think.

But there was someone coming – who was this person? Was it Iarbas, trying to get in and see Dido? No, this was someone she'd never seen before, she was sure of it. He was very tall indeed and covered from head to toe in a long grey cloak. Why would someone wear that if he didn't want to hide something? She shivered. It was very warm, even out here in the garden: what need was there for a long cloak? Well, whoever it was, the guards would stop him. She could see the doorway from where she was sitting. She'd just passed through it herself and she knew that they were both awake and alert . . . Yes, there they stood, one on either side of the doorway, chatting to one another. Because sound carried so far at night, she could even hear their brief bursts of laughter. The tall figure came right up to the guards and passed through into the palace without either of them saying anything. They hadn't even stopped him and asked him who he was and where he thought he was going. If Elissa hadn't been so preoccupied with her own troubles, she might have wondered how this could be, and who it was who could slide into the palace without being challenged, but she was remembering the night she'd spent with Aeneas and the grey man passed swiftly from her mind.

'How is he?' Aeneas was talking quietly, because Ascanius was sleeping now. He'd been feverish and sick and the healer had prescribed a variety of horrible-tasting potions. Elissa had spent the better part of the evening persuading, cajoling, bribing the boy to swallow them, and in the end she'd managed to get most of the medicine down his throat.

'He loved his sleeping potion,' she said. 'It's

flavoured with honey and he was very happy to take it, after those bitter things he's had. He'll sleep soundly now.'

'And you'll get a chance to sleep too, Elissa. You've worked so hard looking after him. I'm grateful to you. You know that, don't you?'

She was sitting at the end of Ascanius' bed. Aeneas was standing next to her, looking at his son. As he spoke, he put out a hand and stroked the top of her head. He said, 'I can relieve you for a while. I'll sleep in there.' He pointed at the small alcove that led off Ascanius' room. For the last two nights Elissa had slept there herself so that she could be within easy reach of the boy, and she offered up a prayer of thanks to the Gods that she'd changed the sheets that morning.

'Thank you,' she said, standing up. 'But my room is very close. You can call me if you need me for anything.'

'Oh, Elissa, if you knew . . .' Aeneas said. 'I wish . . .' He sat down heavily on the bed, but Ascanius was drugged by the sleeping potion and did not stir.

'What? What do you wish?'

'You don't want to know, Elissa. Knowing would upset you. You're so loyal to the queen.'

Elissa said nothing. What could she ask? If I stand here, she thought, he'll either tell me what is worrying him, or not. Even as she hesitated, Aeneas spoke. 'I'm loyal to her as well, but she's difficult, you know? She has her own views about everything and doesn't like being contradicted. And she does *not* understand what you seem to be able to fathom with no problem at all. I have to leave Carthage. Quite soon, I think. But she won't hear of it. And the worst of it is . . .'

Elissa couldn't stop herself. She said: 'Tell me. Tell me the worst of it.'

'She thinks we're married. Man and wife. And we're not . . . We truly are not. I love and revere Dido, but I'm not married to her or tied to her in any way.'

'She says Aphrodite married you. In a cave, up in the mountains.'

Aeneas laughed. 'She needed that as an excuse, that's all. Marriage – especially a marriage sanctioned by a goddess – made what happened in the cave . . . well, *respectable*. I apologize, Elissa. You're too young for this. You're just a child.'

'No, Lord Aeneas, I'm not a child. I wish you wouldn't say that.'

He looked at her then and sighed and said, 'No, you're right. I'm so sorry. No, you're no longer a child, that's sure.' He put out a hand and took hold of her wrist and pulled her gently till she was sitting next to him on the bed. Then he put a hand on her shoulder and pulled her round so that their faces were very close together.

'I could drown in your eyes, Elissa. You have such eyes. Like pools of dark water.'

His hand was still on her shoulder when they kissed. Elissa tried to remember what that felt like and couldn't. Kissing Aeneas was like nothing she'd ever experienced before. A few moons ago he'd touched her lips with his own, and she'd taken out that memory and looked at it so often that she could relive it whenever she felt like it, but this . . . this was like being stunned. Her head swam and her lips opened and it was like . . . like falling, and falling, till he suddenly moved away and lowered his head and took his hand from her shoulder.

'Oh, Elissa, I shouldn't have done that. Please say—'

'I don't mind,' she muttered weakly, hardly able to speak. 'I liked it.'

'And so did I,' Aeneas said. 'But that doesn't stop it from being wrong. I can offer you nothing. And even though you're not a child, I'm certainly too old for you. Go to your bed now, Elissa, before I do something foolish. More foolish than I've done already. Goodnight, dearest girl.'

Elissa went. She needed to lie in her bed and think. Tanith and Nezral were asleep and she was grateful for that. The last thing she wanted was to chatter to those two. She took off her clothes and put on her nightgown, silently. Then she lay on top of her bedclothes and stared at the ceiling. She went over every word Aeneas had spoken. She thought not only about what he'd said but also about the way he'd said it. The feelings he'd shown her were unmistakable. Elissa might not have been as experienced as the other girls when it came to boys, but she knew, she could tell, when a man liked her. Desired her. It wasn't difficult because they never tried to hide it, but rather showed it off.

Even the way Iopas always stared at her, smiled at her, made it clear he thought she was beautiful.

Not only does Aeneas like me, she thought, he's also angry with Dido. He loves her, but they must have had a fight recently. He's been spending so much time away from her. Tonight, for instance, she and Anna had gone to visit a neighbouring rich farmer who had helped them when they first came to Carthage. Elissa started to think about Dido's absence and couldn't stop. The queen was away from the palace. A very long way away.

'Go, child,' said a voice, and she sat up in bed to see who was speaking. 'Listen to Aphrodite.'

'Aphrodite . . . I saw you once, long ago. I thought you were Ascanius' mother. A ghost . . .'

'I'm not a ghost, but I'm here to help you. Come with me.'

Like someone in a dream, Elissa got up from the bed and took the hand the Goddess was offering her. Holding it felt like holding nothing. Aphrodite floated out of the bedroom and Elissa, helpless, walked beside her along the corridor till they came to Ascanius' room. The door stood open. There was a small torch burning high up on one wall, and it threw a warm, pale orange light on to the boy's sleeping face.

'He won't wake up,' Aphrodite whispered. 'I will see to it that he sleeps.'

'But what—?'

'Follow your desires, child. Submit to them,' Aphrodite said, and moved away into the darkness.

Elissa, peering after her, caught a glimpse of floating pale garments, heard the sound of silvery, tinkling bells and felt herself wrapped in the fragrance of roses and almond blossom.

I must be asleep, she thought. I'm sleepwalking. I've come to this room in a dream. *Follow your desires*, the Goddess had said. *Submit to them.*

She tiptoed past Ascanius' bed and went into the alcove. She pulled the curtain that separated the two chambers so that no one could see her. Aeneas was lying half covered by a sheet but she could tell that he was naked. There were his clothes, on the small chest at the end of the bed. He was sleeping deeply. Elissa looked down at him and found it hard to breathe for the love that seemed suddenly to have filled her. She took off the nightgown she was wearing, and trembling all over, she lay down on the narrow bed next to Aeneas. She felt her skin burning where it touched his and their heads were very close together on the pillow. She turned slightly to her right and found his mouth. She didn't even have to move very much to touch it with hers. She lay on her right-hand side and slid her left arm around his waist. He didn't stir at first, and then quite suddenly he opened his eyes. They were level with her own.

'Elissa . . .' he breathed. 'Am I dreaming?'

'I'm dreaming,' she answered, and said, 'Kiss me. Please kiss me.'

'Are you sure? I don't know . . .'

'I know,' she said. 'I know . . .'

That was the last thing she remembered before she felt herself silenced and oblivious of everything except the knowledge that she was holding Aeneas at last in her arms, and they were both overwhelmed; robbed of words and weeping with pleasure.

Before dawn; the palace gardens/the small bedchamber

Thinking back on that night, Elissa remembered other things. How she'd wanted to leave and how he'd stopped her. They hadn't slept at all. Then he'd begged her forgiveness; begged her not to tell Dido; entreated her to forget what had happened between them. She'd promised to say not a word to anyone, and she hadn't until today. But now that Aeneas had gone, she felt no obligation to maintain her silence any longer. If she hid what had happened, that was because it suited her to do so and she wanted to. But, oh, Gods, she had told Iopas and wished fervently that she hadn't. What if he told Anna? He was very close to Dido's sister. What would she say? Or do? Elissa sighed, and standing up, she walked to the pond and let her hand dangle in the cool water. It was time to go back to her bedchamber soon.

She turned towards the palace and was surprised to find Cubby hurrying – almost running – through the garden and calling her name: 'Elissa!'

'Cubby! You've left the bed. What's happened? You look . . . Is something wrong?'

'I don't know. Weird stuff's happening. I saw some-one I didn't know, and when I said *Who goes there?* he didn't listen and just carried right on walking. I don't know who he was. He was very tall—'

'And wearing a long grey cloak with a hood that covered his face. Am I right?'

'Yes! Did you see him too?'

'He walked past me and right into the palace. I've no idea who he was. How odd.'

'Anyway,' said Cubby, 'I've got to go back to the bed. I'm still on guard.'

He squared his shoulders and tried to look tough. Elissa hid her smile.

'Why did you come out here, though? It wasn't to tell me about the man in the grey cloak, was it?'

Cubby hit his head with the flat of his hand. 'I forgot! I was meant to tell you to go and speak to the queen. She's sent for you. You're to go now.'

'Thank you, Cubby. I'm glad you remembered. I wouldn't want to keep her waiting. Especially not tonight.'

'Right,' said Cubby. 'Best hurry then.'

Elissa began to run up the long path towards the doorway of the palace. Cubby followed her, not exactly running but stumbling along as quickly as he could. He was out of breath, but still managed to point to the colonnade across the courtyard. He whispered: 'There he is! See, he's still there. Behind one of the columns. Can you see him?' Cubby peered into the dimness and pointed.

'I see him,' Elissa said, 'but I'm going to leave it to you to find out who he is. I have to go to the queen.'

'Right,' said Cubby. 'I'll try. But he looks a bit scary, don't you think?'

Elissa didn't answer. Her mind was on the queen.

'You sent for me, lady.' Elissa stood in the doorway, hesitant, and with her hair dishevelled.

'Come in, child. Come and sit down and talk to me. It's been such a long night. I'm so tired . . .'

'I can come back if you'd like to sleep.'

'No, no . . . I wish I could but it's impossible. The dreams would be too painful. Being awake is also painful. I can't find any comfort, Elissa. I'm sick with misery. I wish I could close my eyes and sleep for ever and never wake up.'

'Please don't say that, lady. Only Death gives us endless sleep.'

'I'd welcome him. I wish he'd come and take me down into darkness with him. No, don't cry, Elissa dear. I *do* want to talk to you. You comfort me. You're like a daughter to me, you know. The nearest thing to a child I've ever had – do you realize that?'

Elissa nodded. 'And I've thought of you as a kind of mother too, even though a royal one.'

Dido smiled. 'You look well. It's been a pleasant life for you here, hasn't it?'

'Oh, yes! Yes . . .' Elissa said, and wondered how to go on. Why had the queen sent for her? Perhaps it was just what it seemed to be: Dido is lonely and thinks of

224

me kindly, even though she's so unhappy. Elissa felt hot with shame, as though perhaps in this small room the truth about Aeneas and how he had deceived her would come to Dido in a flash of understanding.

'Come and sit beside me, Elissa. I want to ask you something. Do you promise to answer me truthfully?'

Elissa nodded and sat down on the bed, pleating the fabric of her skirt and looking down at her knees. She licked her lips, then started biting the bottom one. Dido was silent and a feeling of dread came over Elissa. She waited and waited and at last the queen began to speak.

'Iopas came to see me,' she said. 'He told me something.'

Elissa felt rage like a mist blinding her. Iopas . . . He'd betrayed her and she thought for a moment that she would scream with fury and misery, but she said nothing. Her fingers went on twisting the material of her skirt and she stared down at them as though they weren't a part of her at all. Dido said, 'D'you want to know what he told me?'

'No, I know what he told you. I mean, I can guess, I think.' It was hard to speak when she was holding herself together, trying not to weep, trying not to scream.

Dido went on: 'He said you're pregnant. Is it true, Elissa?'

Elissa nodded. Dido sighed and went on: 'How long have you known?'

'Not long. A few days really.'

'And you didn't tell me? Or anyone?'

'No. I wasn't . . . I wasn't sure.'

'And now you are.' Dido stood up and went to the window. She'd turned her back on Elissa, who was blinking to stop herself from crying. I'm not going to cry. I can't cry. I won't. But what'll happen now? How can I breathe?

When Dido spoke, it sounded to Elissa as though she too was near to tears. She couldn't even speak aloud, but whispered, 'Who is it? Who is the father?'

'I'd rather not tell you, lady. It's not important. Really, it's better that you don't know.'

Dido whirled round and started screaming at Elissa, hysterical: 'Better! Better for whom, I'd like to know? It's *not* better for me. You randy little bitch! Iopas told me who you'd been with, and I curse the bones and blood and breath and skin of your child. I curse his father, who could lie with my servant when he was married to *me*. To the Queen of Carthage, who would have given him everything. *Everything* . . . And in my palace. You lay with him in *my* palace. What were you thinking of? How could you? You were like my child, Elissa, but now I can't even look at you. Go. I want you to go and never come near me again. I don't want to see you in the palace. Leave. Go to your family in the hills and have your damned baby and I wish you nothing but anguish and sorrow for ever. Go, go.'

Elissa sat stunned, and the tears poured from her eyes and she said nothing. Every bit of her – skin, eyes, nose, hair – *everything* felt scorched, as though Dido's words were fire, burning her. She sobbed and then put a hand over her mouth, and then gasped for air because suddenly she couldn't breathe properly. She couldn't move. Couldn't stand up. Couldn't do anything but sit uselessly on the bed and wish she might die.

For a long time the two women sat in silence. Elissa wanted to go, to leave this small prison of a room and flee to her own bedchamber. But she didn't dare to move till Dido spoke, and the queen showed no sign of wanting to speak.

'Aren't you going to say anything?' Dido asked suddenly. Her voice sounded stronger. Elissa tried to compose herself.

'I don't know what to say.'

'Of course you don't! There are no excuses. How did you dare? After all that I've done for you. I've looked after you and tried to be good to you and even' – Dido's voice wavered a little as she continued – 'thought tenderly of you, as though you were much more to me than a handmaiden. And you do this. Oh, Elissa, if I were stronger I would beat you with my own hands. I'd throw you out of the palace if I had any sense. How *could* you? I thought you were devoted to me. I thought I could trust you, Elissa. How could you add so much pain to the torments I was feeling already?'

'I don't know,' Elissa said. 'I was . . . I couldn't help it. I knew it was wrong. I knew it would hurt you if you found out about us – me and Aeneas.'

'How dare you speak his name and yours in the

same breath?' Dido was shrieking now. 'Are you trying to torture me with every single thing you say? Because that's what you're doing. Go. I don't want to see you ever again. Leave now.'

'Leave the palace? Go back to my parents' home? Oh, please, no, lady. I'd do anything. Anything at all if you'd forgive me. If you'd only let me stay here, in Carthage, I promise you I'd never do anything else to displease you. Please. Tell me what I can do to make matters right between us.'

Dido went to the window and stood with her back to Elissa. 'You'd do anything?' she whispered. 'Would you rid yourself of his child? There are ways.'

Elissa could feel the blood drain away from her face and thought for a moment she was going to faint. She wanted to speak but couldn't. The air seemed to ripple and move in front of her eyes. She had promised the queen. *Anything*, she'd said. If there were words in the world which she might have uttered, Elissa didn't know what they might be. She sank on to the bed and began to weep.

Then, suddenly, Dido was there, sitting next to her; she put an arm around Elissa and began to sob herself. 'Oh, Elissa, listen to me. Listen to my cruelty and cursings – I take them back. I do. I truly do. I'm sorry, sorry, sorry. Forget what I said. What I just said, most of all. I wish you a good life and a good birth and your child nothing but good things. It's not your fault. I understand how it must have been. It was *him*. The bastard Aeneas, who loves nothing and no one but himself and helps himself to any young woman who crosses his path and doesn't care. Doesn't care about anything. I know you love me. You do, don't you? Love me? Stay with me, Elissa. Don't go. I didn't mean it. None of it. I'm crazed. He's made me lose my reason, and I'll never forgive him. It's *him* I curse. May he never know a moment's peace and may the nation he founds be blighted and doomed and never thrive. Carthage will be its enemy for ever. If Aeneas is the beginning of a dynasty, then my people will be the enemies of his people. I vow that on my life, Elissa. You can go. Go to your room. Rest. I'm sorry for what I said. Forgive me.'

Elissa tried to get up but the queen's arms were tight around her neck and she was weeping. 'I forgive you, Elissa. I do. I forgive you everything. I'll miss you so much.'

'But you said I could stay in the palace. Why will you miss me? You said—'

'*Of course* you can stay. I don't know what I'm saying. Weariness has made me mad. Don't listen to me.'

Elissa put her arms up to embrace the queen and they clung together, weeping. At last Dido pulled away and sat up, drying her eyes with the edge of her robe.

'You can see how much I am not myself,' she said, and Elissa understood the effort it cost her to sound normal. 'It's strange, you know. I've never been interested in babies. I've never had any desire to be pregnant. I've seen what it does to a woman's body – how it makes your stomach swell and how lumbering and clumsy you become when you're carrying another human being inside you. The very thought is disgusting. As for birth itself, I've not seen many babies being born, but two or three's quite enough. What's clear is, it's agonizing. The women bellow like cows being slaughtered. There's so much blood and bodily fluids everywhere . . . It's revolting.' She looked at Elissa and smiled. 'I shouldn't be speaking like this about it to you, of course, but I expect you've seen birth and know just as well as I do what's involved.'

Elissa nodded. 'Yes,' she said, and was wondering whether she ought to tell Dido about the visit of Artemis and her promise of help with the birth when the queen went on: 'Until quite recently, when I imagined myself in that posture, with my legs apart and screaming like a stuck boar, I told myself that I'd never, never submit to such torture. But then, after my marriage, those feelings just vanished.'

Dido glanced at Elissa. 'Since that day, I've wanted Aeneas' child to fill my body; to grow within me. Isn't that odd? I don't fear giving birth any longer. I was ready to go through any pain. I would have been brave. And you do hear stories of easy deliveries. Some women find the process completely painless and untroubling. I collected countless tales of peasants who gave birth in the fields and then picked themselves up and went on gathering in the crops.'

Elissa stood up. 'If you give me permission, lady, I'll leave you now.'

Dido said nothing, but waved her hand in a gesture of dismissal and Elissa fled.

She ran down the corridors till she came to Iopas'
chamber. Without knocking, she flung open the door,
and seeing him sitting at his table writing away on a
parchment as though he'd done nothing inflamed her
to such an extent that she began to shout as soon as
she was in the room.

'Iopas, how could you do such a thing? Don't speak.
I don't want to hear your excuses. I wish I had the
strength to hit you, to fight you. If I were a man, I'd
beat you with my fists and bite you and kick you and
spit on you when I'd finished. How did you dare to
betray my secret? I thought you were my friend. I
thought . . . Oh, what does it matter what I thought?
It's not true, any of it. What matters is what's happened. You . . . *you*, Iopas, have ruined everything. My
life, Dido's life, everything. She's so hurt. Did you
know that she wanted a baby with Aeneas? How do
you think knowing about me makes her feel? And me
– how do you think I feel? Why do you sit there and say
nothing?'

'I can't say anything because you haven't let me utter
a single word since you came bursting into my room.
Did I give you permission to come in? I don't
remember you even asking. You just barged in.'

'I'm entitled to barge in. How do *you* feel, Iopas?'
Elissa sat down heavily on the stool beside Iopas' work
table. 'Are you sorry for what you did? What you told
the queen? Of course you aren't. Those who tell the
truth are always praised, even though their truth is a
body blow to the person hearing it. I don't know what

231

to say now. I'm powerless. I can't do anything. I'm . . .
I feel sick all the time. I'm frightened of what's going
to happen to me – and to my baby. What's Dido
going to say when she comes out of that room? She'll
get rid of me, I know. She's sad now, and weeping for
Aeneas, but one day she'll be herself again and then
she won't be able to watch me . . . the child growing
inside me. She'll banish me. I will be nothing but a
reminder of Aeneas and she won't be able to bear it.
That's what I think, and I blame you, Iopas.'

'I accept the blame, Elissa. And you're right. It was
. . . I wasn't thinking. It was an unkind thing to do. If I
had the time over again, I wouldn't tell Dido. What you
say is true. I've made it impossible for you to stay here
and so I'm punishing myself as well, Elissa. That's my
excuse, if you want one. I did it because – well, you can
guess.'

'You think you're in love with me, or some nonsense
like that.'

'It's a funny thing . . .' Iopas smiled at her. 'When
you're in love with Aeneas (which, in my opinion,
takes the laurels for the most unsuitable falling in love
ever), then it's real and beautiful and can't be
criticized because it's true love. The same for our
beloved queen. Her love is sanctified and blessed and
everyone has to tiptoe around her because she's been
deserted by her husband. Who never even *was* her
husband, not properly, from what I heard. The whole
thing's in her head, but because she's the queen, the
rest of us have to gather round and comfort her. I

don't *mind* comforting her, you understand, because I'm a believer in love. A follower of Aphrodite. Her servant for ever. And I'm also devoted to Dido. Then there's Anna. I have to be polite to her even though what I want to do is tell her never to talk to me again, but she loves me, and because she's the queen's sister and I can't afford to upset her, I have to be . . . well, understanding. I'm sick to death of it. But if I'm supposed to be sympathetic to you and to her, and to her sister too, then I demand some sympathy from you.' Iopas stood up and went to kneel in front of Elissa. 'You must believe me. I want to hear from your lips that you believe me when I tell you how much I love you.'

'I'm not discussing your love. I don't give a fig for it. I'll never love you and you might as well know that. I can't trust you. I don't even like you very much. I'm going. Don't try and follow me. I want to be by myself. You're nothing but a sneaky, wretched, horrible person and I'd be happy not to see you ever again.'

'You're tired, Elissa,' Iopas said. 'You're not yourself. I don't blame you for being angry. You'll see things differently when you're more rested.'

Elissa couldn't find any words that would be suitably withering, so she said nothing and left the room. Gods, the conceit of him! He was nothing but a worm. A snake. A monster. How did he dare to address her as though she were a stupid child who didn't know what she was saying? Oh, if only she were a boy! She'd soon show him what being bruised and battered meant!

Anna

First light; the small bedchamber

Anna sat beside her sister, wringing her hands and trying hard not to cry. She had not slept all night and she felt bruised in every part of her body, as though someone had been pummelling her flesh for hours. What Iopas had told her was like a brand on her skin. Thinking of him and Elissa together was like taking a dagger and piercing herself with it, over and over again. She said, 'I know about Elissa. Iopas told me. Oh, Dido, I can't bear it.' She began weeping and used the corner of her scarf to wipe her eyes. 'I'm sorry . . . I know you're not interested in my feelings at this moment and I can understand, but oh, the pain is unbearable. Iopas and Elissa . . . together. And a child . . .' Anna's body shook with sobs.

'Iopas?' Dido spoke angrily. 'He told me about Elissa's pregnancy, it's true, and I suppose he's now told you, because you clearly know, but he's not the father.'

'He must be . . .' Anna murmured. 'Who else could it be? I know that Iopas loves her. It's been . . . I'd given up real hope that Iopas and I—'

'It's not Iopas.'

'Who then?'

'Fool! Aeneas. My Aeneas. That's who it is.'

Anna's eyes widened and she sat up very straight. Dido shouted: 'You look like a goldfish with your mouth gaping open . . . You're a fool, but now at least you can be happy. Your precious Iopas is innocent and you can continue trying to lure him into your bed. Much good may it do you. *You* should be comforting *me*, Anna. Can you imagine the agony I feel? If some-one with a knife were to come in now and slice off pieces of my skin, it would be a welcome distraction from the pain I feel. Do you understand my pain? How could you? Everything I taste and breathe is bitter. I can't bear it. I could've lived with anything – *anything* – but Aeneas' child – the child he refused to give me – in Elissa's womb. How will I be able to look at it? How can I watch her, growing and swelling and reminding me with every day more and more of what the two of them did? And where did they do it, Anna? I can't stop asking myself. Wondering. In her bed? No, impossible. She shares her quarters with other girls. Where then? In the garden? In the bathhouse? I can't stop seeing the two of them naked together – they pass in front of my eyes and I rub and rub at them to rid myself of the sight, but oh, Gods, Anna, it goes on and on, and what I see in my imagination is more and more vivid till I can see them writhing. I can hear— *No!*' Dido screamed and fell forward on to the cushions, burying her head in them. 'I can't . . . take these pictures away. Take out my eyes. I don't know how . . . I want to die. Let me die. Oh, Gods, let me stop *seeing*—'

'Dido! Beloved sister . . . don't. Don't do this. You'll fall ill. Take a sip of this sleeping draught. Let me bring you some more wine. Rest. Don't cry. Please, please, stop, my lovely sister. Look at you . . . Stop . . .'

Anna fell silent, not knowing what else to say. She had been relieved at first to learn that Iopas had not . . . was not . . . what she'd thought he was. But the truth was even worse, she realized. He must hate me, to trick me like that. He let me think he was the father of Elissa's child only to hurt me. He did it on purpose. He hates me, she thought. I will never speak to him again. Never. It was as though a weight of darkness had settled on her shoulders. She sat near Dido, stroking her back, muttering soothing sounds and almost weeping herself. I don't know what I can do for either of us, she thought. I don't know how to make everything that's tormenting her go away. Fade. Disappear. I can't help her and I can't help myself.

Then, just as suddenly as she'd dissolved in misery on the cushions, Dido sat up again. She took the corner of her robe and wiped her eyes with it. She turned to Anna and said, 'I've decided what must be done. I want you to go down to the harbour. Now. I want you to stay there, where Aeneas can see you, until he has sailed, and then you can come back here and tell me about his departure. Will you do that?'

'Now? You want me to go now?' Anna put an arm around her sister and hugged her, relieved that at last the storm of weeping was over. Perhaps Dido had lived through the worst of her pain and would feel less sorrowful from this moment. She said, 'Can't I wait till the sun is a little higher in the sky?'

'No. I want you to go now.'

'But why? What makes you think Aeneas'll be looking at the shore anyway? He'll be busy setting sail. I could try and speak to him if you like, but he wouldn't want to speak to me, would he? Let him go and let his fate be as the Gods decree. It's nothing to do with us any longer. If I'm honest, I think you've taken leave of your senses.'

'I haven't, Sister.' Dido smiled. 'I believe I'm seeing clearly for the very first time. I will order up a small detachment of soldiers to accompany you and I want you to go and stand in the harbour master's house – just where we stood when we saw him come ashore, d'you remember that day? – and watch the ships leaving. Then you can come back and tell me about it.'

'Why don't you go? If you're so anxious to see Aeneas drifting away, then *you* go down there.'

'You're a fool, Anna. How can I go? You have to be my eyes. It would be undignified for me to run down to the harbour as if I were a . . . serving wench or—' Dido suddenly stiffened. Covering her mouth with the fingers of one hand, she began to moan and rock backwards and forwards.

237

'Oh, Dido, stop.' Anna put her arms around her sister. 'Don't make such sounds, my dearest sister. It hurts me to hear them. I'll go. I will. Straight away. Anything I can do to make you happier, I'll do. You know that. You must, I suppose, have reasons I know nothing about . . . I'll go. I will watch him leaving our shores and come back to tell you about it.'

'You don't know how grateful I am,' Dido said. 'You are the one person in the world whom I can trust. You've been – you are – the best sister. The very best. I love you, Anna.'

Anna brushed tears from her eyes as she stood up. 'You've never said that, Dido. Not ever. Though of course I've always known that you love me. Sisters don't have to say the words to one another. Who doubts a sister's devotion? I love you too, Dido. You know that.'

'I wish . . .'

'What? What do you wish, Dido?'

'It doesn't matter, Anna. Go now. I want you to go.'

Anna hurried away to do her sister's bidding. Everything she saw had the glow of early dawn about it. How beautiful the city was in the pearly light! Well, she would go and find the guards and get down to the harbour. How I long to see him sail out of our waters, she told herself. Perhaps Dido will be peaceful and happy once he's gone. And Iopas? He was nothing but a pretty young man who wanted to hurt her. But Elissa didn't love him and that was good. Perhaps this was a punishment from Aphrodite, and if it was, then it was precisely what he deserved.

Cubby

The sky streaked with light; the courtyard

'Boy! Wake up, boy!'

Cubby opened his eyes and was so amazed to see Dido standing over him that he mumbled and muttered as he struggled to his feet.

'I'm sorry . . . not s'posed to go to sleep. Sorry.'

'Don't apologize, boy. What's your name?'

'Cubby. Everyone calls me Cubby.'

'But you must have a real name. Will you not tell me what it is? You deserve to be known by it for the care you've taken, standing guard all night.'

'It's Akbar, lady.'

The queen smiled. 'Well, Akbar, I'm sorry to wake you. But I want you to do something for me. Something most important. Can you do it?'

Cubby thought about this for some moments, then said, 'I suppose it depends. What it is, I mean. There's some stuff I couldn't do for you. But I'd try.' No, you fool, he told himself. That's not how you're supposed

239

to talk to the queen. He added, 'I'd be honoured, my lady,' and hoped that was a bit better. More respectful and polite. Dido didn't seem angry so he reckoned it was.

She said, 'You must go to the guards standing at the main entrance and tell them to go back to their quarters and sleep. They must be exhausted. As you are, I can see. When you've told them my wishes, you too can go to your room.'

'But . . .'

'But what?' Dido was frowning and Cubby worried that he'd said something *really* wrong.

'Why would the guards listen to anything I tell them? Maybe I should find the master of the guard?'

'No, don't do that, Akbar. I want you to go. Here' – she pulled a ring off her finger and gave it to Cubby, who nearly dropped it – 'show them that. It's the royal seal – can you see? Tell them I've given it to you – you are carrying a part of my power. D'you understand?'

Cubby nodded, too overcome to speak. *Akbar . . .* He'd never get used to being called that. He was Cubby, and that was all there was to it. He clutched the ring tight so as not to lose it. The circle of gold was heavy in his hand and he found himself for some reason he couldn't quite understand with tears in his eyes. That was bad. That wasn't brave. He stood up straighter and hoped that no girlish drops were about to fall from his eyes.

'I'll bring it back to you here, right?' he said, his voice only slightly wobbly.

'Keep it, Akbar. Keep it and remember me.'

'Yes, my lady.' What did she mean? Why would he forget her when she lived here and he saw her quite often? He knew he found it hard to hang on to some stuff in his head but no one could forget the queen. She was too beautiful. Too kind. And now she'd made him important. More important than the master of the guard.

'You should go now,' she said. 'Don't delay. I want those guards fast asleep as soon as possible.'

'Yes, my lady.' He bowed deeply from the waist and turned and began to walk away as quickly as he could. When he got to the doorway, he was surprised to find the two guards leaning against the columns with their eyes closed. He coughed and their eyes immediately flew open and they stood to attention.

'Bloody hell, Cubby! Whatcha creeping around like that for?' said one of them. 'Aren't you s'posed to be guarding the bed in the courtyard?'

'Not any more. The queen sent me to tell you you can go. Back to your quarters. You can go to sleep is what I mean. What *she* means, I mean.'

'As if! The queen talking to the likes of you? Maybe I'm still asleep and dreaming this. Gotta be that.'

'No, look.' Cubby didn't blame the guard for his words. It *was* a bit unbelievable, the idea that the queen would give her orders through someone like him. He didn't properly believe it himself. He held out his open hand with the ring lying on it. 'This is the queen's ring. I told her you wouldn't believe me and she gave me this. To show you.'

'Bloody Hades! It *is* the royal seal too. You sure you've not just stolen this?'

'No, of course I haven't. The queen gave it to me, I told you already.' Tears pricked in Cubby's eyes and he blinked rapidly to stop them from falling. Guards didn't cry. Not for any reason. They just didn't. He said: 'If she finds you haven't obeyed her orders, she'll be upset. Cross. You should go now.'

'Not arguing with you, mate,' said the soldier. 'Could do with a bit of kip and that's a fact. Feels as though I've been here for ever. Come on, you.' He prodded his companion in the ribs and the two of them slouched away in the direction of the guards' quarters. Cubby watched them go. I'm the only guard left now, he thought. I'm not going to bed, even though the queen said I could.

He sat down on one of the stone benches set on either side of the doorway and leaned his back against the wall. He slipped the ring on to one of his fingers. Would he be allowed to wear it? Wouldn't everyone think he'd stolen it? They would, but then the queen can put them right, he told himself. She can say: *I gave that to Akbar*, and everyone'd have to believe her. She'd have to explain to them who Akbar was, but she could do that. They'd believe her. They might even start calling him that too. Akbar. He was starting to like the sound of it.

He fell asleep almost at once. Then he had a dream. That woman – Aphrawhatsit – the beautiful one he'd seen on the hunt and when they'd first brought the bed into the courtyard – was here again, and what's more, sitting right next to him. Should he say something? Maybe better not.

'I can't prevent it,' she said. 'Even the Gods are powerless sometimes. My son is sailing out of the harbour because that's his destiny. He couldn't stay here. And Dido – Dido has her fate too. I've tried to prevent it. Now we have to wait.'

'Wait? What for?' Cubby thought: I'm talking in my sleep.

'For things to come to pass, boy. Look down there.'

'D'you mean the tall man in the grey cloak. I've seen him before. He coming here?'

'Of course. He has an appointment with the queen. I wish I could turn him away. I can't.'

'Well,' said Cubby, trying to sound cheerful; to console this pretty lady, who was looking a bit teary-eyed. 'Maybe she's looking forward to seeing him. Maybe he's a friend of hers.'

'Don't say that! How *dare* you say that!' She stood up then and drifted away. Her skirts floated around her ankles and there was that tinkling noise again he remembered from before. Those silver bells sewn on her clothes. And the lovely smell. But why was she so angry? Cubby had no idea and was too tired to work it out.

'Keep your hair on!' he shouted after her. 'I've not done anything wrong.'

Elissa

The sun rising; the maidservants' bedchamber/Dido's bedchamber/Iopas' bedchamber/the courtyard

'Wake up, Elissa. Listen to me. Oh, please wake up, child!'

'I'm awake. What is it? What do you want? Oh . . .' Elissa struggled to sit up, still half asleep but realizing all at once that it wasn't either Tanith or Nezral or even the Lady Anna who was pulling at her gown, but Hera, the queen of all the Goddesses on Olympus. 'Am I still asleep? Is it you, Hera?'

'Of course it's me, girl. There's no time to lose. You must go at once. I need your help. Dido needs your help.'

'Why, what's the matter?'

Instead of answering, the Goddess sat down on Elissa's bed and tears began to flow from her eyes. She gathered her cloak, trimmed with peacock feathers, around her shoulders and Elissa thought she looked more like a sad old woman than an inhabitant of

244

Olympus. Hera said, 'There's nothing more I can do. I can only send you to help her and see to it that she doesn't suffer too much. Go, go to Dido's chamber – the royal bedchamber, not the little room she's been hiding in . . . She's there choosing garments to wear for this day.'

'Then she must feel better,' Elissa said, and got out of bed. 'If she's dressing.'

'That depends on what she is dressing for,' Hera said. 'What occasion.'

'Is there to be a special occasion?'

'Don't ask so many questions. Just go. Go and be beside her, I beg of you. Help her as much as you can. Remember that I'm there, watching you both, even if you can't see me. I will come with you as far as the queen's door.'

Elissa left her room, aware of the Goddess floating beside her. When they reached Dido's bedchamber, they found it closed.

'Shall I knock? What shall I do?' Elissa asked.

'Take this feather and I will open the door. Step inside and say nothing. Dido will neither see nor hear us, but we will see her and her companion.'

Elissa was about to say, *What companion?* when the door to the chamber swung open and she shrank back, chilled with terror. The tall man in the long grey cloak was there, with his hood pulled over his face so that his features were hidden. The queen was speaking to him.

'I remember you,' she said, looking up at him. 'I saw you once before. As I walked up from the harbour on the day my lord arrived in the city. Who are you? How did you get past my guards? How dare you come into my room without my permission? And take that hood off if you want to speak to me.'

'There are not many who can look at my face, but you are capable of it.' The voice that came from the folds of the cloak was low and grating, as though speech was difficult. 'I am Hades, God of Death. Good and bad, everyone comes to me in the end.'

Elissa trembled as white, bony hands pushed back the hood of the grey cloak. She saw how Dido flinched as she stared at the black beard and the hollow cheeks. The God had so little flesh on his bones that you could see his skull quite clearly. His eyes were dark and shadowed and had no flicker of life in them. Elissa thought that looking into them would be like falling into a bottomless well. An icy mist clung to Hades' figure and drifted into every part of the room.

Dido gave a mirthless laugh. 'I'm not frightened of you, you know. Indeed, I find myself drawn to you. Will you kiss me? I long for your cold white mouth on mine. Has anyone ever said such words to you before?'

'Multitudes. There are many who seek me out. Who love me.'

'I could love you now,' Dido said. 'I long to come with you. Take me in your arms and kiss me. Give me your hand and I will follow.'

'It is almost time. We will meet again, you may be sure, Dido. And in the meantime, a kiss to seal the promise of your love for me.'

Hades bent his head and Elissa saw the God kiss Dido, who flinched and cried out but who nevertheless leaned in towards him, almost swooning against his chest. She put out her hand to touch his face. He stroked the queen's hair, then turned and walked away. At once the warmth of the night returned and Dido went back to sit on the bed. She covered her eyes with her hands.

Elissa came forward, dropping the peacock feather on the floor. 'Lady, I have come to help you dress – to help you choose what to wear.'

'Who told you to come? How did you know I was here? I'm perfectly well able to choose something by myself . . .'

Elissa was about to tell the queen about Hera but it was clear that Dido had forgotten she'd even asked the question. She stood by the chest that held her finest robes and threw it open.

'Once,' she said, 'when I was a very small girl, in my native city of Tyre, snow fell on the high ground. Do you know what snow is? No, how could you know?'

'I've seen it,' Elissa said. 'You forget that I was born in a mountain village. I remember it.'

'I loved it. We children ran out and scooped up handfuls of the soft, white, wet stuff. I put some in my mouth to taste it. The cold made my lips numb and yet they burned at the same time: isn't that strange? Well, now I've felt it again. I've found someone new to love me, Elissa. Better than Aeneas. His kiss is like an icy branding iron and he's marked me. I'm his for ever now.'

Dido began to take out the clothes in the chest and lay them on the bed. She moved, Elissa noticed, slowly and languidly, as though swimming in the air. She said, 'Sit down, Elissa. You can't simply stand over there like a statue. Come here and sit on the bed and help me to dress.'

Elissa obeyed and Dido went on speaking. 'I've been silent for most of the night, Elissa. I'm tired of keeping my thoughts to myself. My dearest sister left me a phial of the healer's sleeping draught and soon, very soon, I will sleep, but not yet. There it is, on the table over there. I've been turning over in my mind what I will do now that Aeneas is no longer here in Carthage. I could go back to my life as it was before he arrived, couldn't I?'

Elissa nodded eagerly. 'No one would blame you. Your people would still love you just the same.'

'Yes, but they would *speak*. I am the queen, and everyone at court, in the city, in the countryside beyond – my friends and allies, my enemies and detractors – they'd all have opinions and they wouldn't be slow to voice them. Can't you just imagine it? Listen: *She was bamboozled, just like any serving wench. Couldn't keep her legs together, and look what happens? He leaves her, doesn't he? And she's high and dry. And that's not all. Not by a long chalk. He's been meddling with her maid too, and guess what? That chubby child – yes, the maid's kid – that's Aeneas' work. No doubt. I wonder that she lets the child have the run of the palace. Generous but stupid, I call it.*'

'Don't say such things, my lady,' Elissa cried, tears

beginning to gather in her eyes. 'Please . . .' Dido had adopted a stupid voice, a common accent, like the lowest of the servants. She thought: I won't stay here if that's what she's going to keep on doing – being unkind to me.

'You can't leave her,' Hera whispered in Elissa's ear. 'Remember all I told you. She needs you, Elissa.'

Dido clearly hadn't heard anything. She was still speaking, half to Elissa and half to herself. 'I couldn't bear it, d'you understand? Whispers wherever I went. Sideways looks. The disgusting *pity* on every face. *Poor Dido.* Even if I were to send you back to your village – oh Gods, don't look at me like that, child. I have no intention of sending you anywhere. But imagine if I did, how the gossips would prattle and there'd be no way of hiding the truth. What am I saying? I'm not myself. You know that I love you . . . Elissa – why should you be punished when I myself lost what little sense I had in Aeneas' presence? Why should I blame you when I too have been acting like a lovesick fool? And then, even worse, more wounding than the voices of the living would be the memories of the dead. What will historians and poets say about me? What will they write? What'll remain carved on tablets of stone? You don't think that matters but it does, and I know exactly how the story will be presented.'

Dido sank on to the bed and hid her head in her hands.

'Say something to her,' Hera whispered. 'Anything.'

'How?' Elissa asked. 'How will it be presented?'

'It'll be written by men. I won't be important enough to merit a mention on my own account. No, it'll be a brief appearance in tales of Aeneas' bright journey to fame and power. To triumph. *The great leader, Aeneas, stopped in Carthage on his way to found a powerful nation and fell in love briefly with the queen, whose name was Dido.* That's what they'll say. Unless I make the story mine. And I have the power to do that. I have a way of changing everything. And I will do it, I promise you, Elissa.'

'Are you looking for a particular dress, lady?' Elissa asked.

'I've found it. The robes I wore on the day of the hunt. The robes that I was married in. Here. Help me take off this rag.'

Elissa stepped forward and eased the soiled garment over the queen's head. It was damp with the sweat of the night, and torn where Dido's nails must have plucked at it.

'Throw it away, Elissa.' Dido kicked the dress from where it lay on the floor at her feet into the furthest corner of the room. 'Give me the white robes . . . Yes, that's good. And now I must have a crown. I need a crown.'

'Shall I comb your hair, lady?' How could the queen place a crown over this dishevelled mop of tangled curls? It would look ridiculous. 'Please sit here and let me attend to it.'

Dido sighed. 'Very well, child,' she said. 'If you like. It makes no difference to me.'

Elissa picked up the comb, carved from a single piece of ivory, and began to draw it through the mass of hair. Slowly, gently, she teased apart the knots and tangles, and Dido closed her eyes. She might fall asleep as I work, Elissa thought, and was careful not to pull or hurt the queen in any way. There was silence in the bedchamber, but for Dido's quiet breathing.

'Aren't you finished yet?' she said suddenly, sitting up abruptly. 'Surely it's done by now?'

'Well enough,' Elissa said. She gathered all the hair together into a knot at the nape of Dido's neck and fastened this with an ebony clasp.

'Thank you, Elissa.' Dido stood up and went to the jewel chest that stood in a corner of her chamber, where her most prized treasures were kept. Now, carelessly, the lid was flung open and the soft leather pouches containing the queen's most precious gems were thrown on to the bed as though they were worthless. Dido bent down and took out her best headdress: a circle of gold set with amber, lapis lazuli and pearls; with topazes, emeralds and chalcedony.

'Sychaeus gave me this on our wedding day,' she said, 'and I'm wearing it to spite Aeneas. You know what I'd say to him if he were here?'

Elissa shook her head. How can I go on and on listening to Dido mourning Aeneas? she asked herself. Doesn't she realize how I'm feeling? How much I'm missing him? Just as much as she is, only with no one to help me and comb my hair and make me feel better.

All alone. No one cares about me. No one remembers that I loved him too.

'That's because you are a child and not royal and have only come into this story by accident,' Hera whispered, and Elissa shivered. The Goddess could read her mind. 'Aphrodite chose to meddle as usual. She never knows when to leave something alone. She can't resist the opportunity to spread love around. It causes nothing but trouble but she will not be told, and we, the rest of us, have to pick up the pieces. Answer the queen. Go on, child.'

'What would you say to Aeneas?' Elissa said.

'I'd say: *See, once I was married to a man who knew my worth.*' Dido turned and took up the phial containing the sleeping draught from where she'd placed it, on top of another chest. 'I will drink this in a moment, Elissa. Will you carry it for me? We must go and find Iopas and wake him.'

'Why?' The word burst out of her before she could stop herself.

Dido paused and looked at her and for the first time seemed to see Elissa as someone suffering separately from her. She sank on to a stool and tears flowed out of her eyes and ran unchecked down her cheeks. 'Oh, Elissa, I'd forgotten. Forgotten how you must be feeling . . . I'm so sorry. But I have no room in my thoughts for anything but what I have to do, and I need Iopas to write something for me.' Dido came to Elissa and flung her arms around the girl. 'I know you love me and want to help me and I am grateful. Remember that, Elissa. But you can't write. I need Iopas for that.'

'I don't understand—' Elissa began, but Dido had already pulled away from their embrace and started to walk down the corridor towards Iopas' room. Where were they going? What would Iopas have to write down? And why?

'The sleeping draught,' Dido said, pausing. 'Do you have it with you?'

Elissa nodded and raised the phial a little so that Dido could see it, and they continued through the darkened corridors to Iopas' room. Dido knocked at his door and pushed it open when there was no answer. Elissa almost smiled to see how flustered he looked, how unkempt, woken from a deep sleep. When he saw the queen, his eyes widened and he sat up and apologized and mumbled and also, Elissa could see, was trying to work out what exactly she was doing there.

'I'm sorry to wake you from your slumber, Iopas, but I need you. Get dressed at once, bring your writing materials and meet me in the courtyard, please.'

'Yes, my lady,' Iopas said, but the queen had hurried away and Elissa went after her, towards the courtyard. On their way, Dido picked up one of the torches still burning on the wall. She held it in front of her as she went.

'Wait, my lady...' Iopas was running after them. Elissa reflected that he must have got dressed more quickly than ever in his life before. 'Where are we going?' He spoke to Elissa but she didn't answer. She had no words for him and wished he didn't have to be here.

'Did you bring parchment? A pen? Ink?' Dido said.

'Yes – my writing box. But—'

'Don't ask questions.'

When they reached the courtyard, Dido said, 'Can you sit on a bench here and write? Is that possible?'

Iopas smiled. 'I can write anywhere.' How superior and smug he sounds, Elissa thought. What is Dido doing? Why does he have to write?

'Then begin: *Dearest Sister,*' said Dido.

'*Dearest Sister . . .*'

'Iopas, if you repeat my words, we'll be here too long. Just write. Say nothing.'

Dido put the torch she was carrying into the mouth of one of the urns, where it blazed in the light of the new dawn. '*Do not be sad for me, Anna. I know what I'm doing. I've decided to put an end to my life.*'

'*No!*' Elissa shouted, and ran forward, and Iopas dropped his pen and leaped from his seat.

'Elissa, be silent! Sit down, Iopas, and know your place. Elissa, dearest, I know you care for me but you can't tell me whether I may die or not. I'm sorry for the pain I'm causing you, but I have to stop my own agony. I am the Queen of Carthage and must do what I think best. Iopas, please write.'

Iopas sat down, and his hand trembled so much that Elissa wondered how he would continue. How can I stop her? she asked herself. How can she throw away her life? Why?

'Do not cry, Elissa,' said Hera, and suddenly the Goddess was in front of her, wiping her tears away with the end of a peacock feather. She held Elissa's chin in one hand as she did so and turned her face from one side to another.

'My mother held me just like that,' she told Hera. 'She wiped my tears away just as you are doing.'

'You'll need all your courage to watch what is coming,' Hera answered. 'And Dido will need you to help her. You cannot weep, however sad you feel. You have to stand beside her.'

'I will. I will. I'll be brave, I promise.'

'And I shall do all I can too.' Hera stroked Elissa's cheeks with her fingers and sighed and vanished into the shadows around the courtyard.

Dido was still speaking to Iopas. She said, 'Listen to my words, Iopas, as I dictate them to you. They're meant for everyone, not just for my poor sister, who is the one person who'll miss me.'

'No, lady, we'll all miss you . . . really. I mean . . .'

'You'll recover. So will you, Elissa. Anna may not. I don't mean to hurt her. I want to leave her some consolation. Death's so easy for the one who chooses it, and so hard for those they leave behind. So hard. I'm being selfish, I know that. I don't care. I have to look after myself, Iopas. My reputation.'

'Your reputation stands high, lady.'

'It does today. Tomorrow, if I humbly submit to this treatment – this desertion, this betrayal – it will be lowered. I'll become like every other woman whose man has left her. I can't . . . can't allow that to happen. Please write: *You've been the best of sisters and I know that my kingdom will be safe while you live. See to it that you marry someone who will help you to care for Carthage. Be a friend to Elissa. It's not her fault, but I can't live in the same world, let alone the same palace, as a child whose father is Aeneas. If it falls to you to tell him of my death, say that I curse his kingdom with my dying words and wish for our two nations to be forever at war. May his forces be brought low and his lands overrun by enemies. And may he fear the hour of his own death, for I will be waiting for him in Hades and he will not escape my curse. My death won't be painful; rather a way to stop the pain that has been tearing me apart. Continue to love me, Anna, as I will love you from beyond the grave. Remember me.*

'I'll write my own name, Iopas. I have to sign it myself. I've given my royal seal away and there's no time to fetch another.'

She leaned over the parchment and wrote on it the letters of her name. Then she took the torch out of the urn and raised it above her head.

'My thanks to you, Iopas. You should go now.'

'Let me stay, lady. I beg you, let me stay.'

'You won't like what you see.'

'Nevertheless,' he said, with a break in his voice, 'I have to see it. To bear witness. So that I can write the truth and everyone will know.'

'Very well. On one condition.'

'Anything.'

'Go over there – beside the fourth column. Do not

move from there in any circumstances. Do you agree to do that? Do you promise? *In any circumstances.* Whatever you see.'

Iopas' face, Elissa noticed, was white. 'I promise, lady. I give you my word.'

'Good. I'm grateful to you, Iopas. Stand like a statue. Remember you've given your word.'

Elissa watched as Iopas walked unsteadily to his position beside the fourth column. Dido turned to her and said, 'Where is the sleeping draught, Elissa? Where is the phial?'

'Here, lady. In my hand.'

'Then give it to me.'

Elissa handed the little bottle to the queen, who removed the stopper and took a sip of the liquid.

'It tastes of poppies and honey. Drowsy. I feel drowsy. I must lie on my bed again. Our bed. Oh, Elissa, this bed . . .'

Dido sank to her knees and leaned against it. 'Hand me the torch, child,' she said, and because her head was almost buried in the clothes that hung from the end of the bed, Elissa thought she must have misheard.

'The torch? You want the torch?'

'Do not hand it to her, girl,' said a voice like knives being drawn across a stone. 'That is for me to do.'

Elissa recognized Hades, standing beside her in his grey cloak, with his head uncovered. She shrank from the God, frozen by the chill mist that surrounded him. His eyes burned black fire in the hollows of his skull and the hand that he held out for the torch was nothing but white bones. Hades grasped the burning torch and turned to the queen.

'Come, Dido. Stand up. Give me your hand.'

Dido rose from the ground and said, smiling, 'Oh, Hades, how I've longed to see you. You'll never desert me. Stay with me. Help me.'

'I will. I'll take care of you now.'

Elissa couldn't move. She wasn't sure whether what she saw was happening, or whether she was in a kind of wakeful dream. The God held the torch to the clothes on the bed, and bright tongues of fire began to lick at the wood and leap and shine and move through what was piled on the mattress, and she saw one thing after another begin to glow and burn and flicker and blossom into glowing flowers that spread and billowed and turned into sheets of flame. After a while Elissa could scarcely make out where the queen was. She peered through the smoke and caught a glimpse of Dido's face. Her eyes were closed and she was lying as though asleep on a pile of silky cushions. Perhaps she feels nothing, Elissa told herself. Perhaps she's already dead. Hades is with her. He must help her. Tears fell from Elissa's eyes and she sank to her knees near the bed. 'Please, kind Hades,' she sobbed, 'help her feel no pain. Let it be a soft bed for her.' Perhaps she imagined it, but she could hear Hades speaking.

'Take the sword, Dido,' he said. 'Aeneas' sword will cut the swiftest path to my kingdom. Don't wait for the fire.'

How will she hold the sword? Elissa wondered. She's too weak. She's fainted away. She may even have died already. All at once the smoke cleared and there was Hades, standing over Dido like a lover, and Elissa could see the blade of Aeneas' sword shining so brightly that her eyes hurt from the shining, and she closed them, and in her head she heard the queen's voice saying: *Do it. Plunge the blade into my heart. I want you to. Please, dearest Hades, take me to your kingdom*, and there was a single terrible cry, shrill and sharp as a stabbing sword, and it must be Dido shrieking, Elissa thought, and she cried out too with the sorrow of it, and then she covered her head with her arms and rocked from side to side, and beside her the bed and everything that was on it flared and blazed and roared with the voice of fire, and just as Elissa was about to turn and run away from everything, she heard someone speaking, and the words sounded cool and sweet and like no other words she'd ever heard, as though each one were coated with silver and honey and soothed your ear as you heard it.

'I have come, Dido,' said this voice. 'I am Iris, Hera's messenger. She has always looked to your care. I will take your soul to the Elysian Fields, dear Queen. Rest now. There will be no more pain. Never again. See, I am cutting a lock of your hair to free you of your body for ever.'

Elissa watched as Iris' wide, wide, opalescent wings beat a soft rhythm, and then it seemed to her that Dido was being lifted up and carried: encircled and held tight, soaring and safe. Hera's messenger flew up and up and out of the palace, and a stream of glowing sparks fell to earth behind her. Behind them. Is that truly Dido she's bearing in her arms? Elissa asked herself. Or perhaps I'm imagining it and the poor queen's body is still there, nothing but ashes now and blackened bones. A bitter taste rose in her mouth and the tears flowed from her eyes unchecked. The bed, devoured by leaping ribbons of scarlet and gold, was already reduced to a pile of blackened wood. Looking up, Elissa saw something like a scarf of shimmering fabric drop from the sky, and she knew, with complete certainty, that this was Dido's life leaving her body and falling to the ground in gentle folds as Iris carried her away to the Elysian Fields.

She tried to speak, but every word she'd ever known had vanished from her mouth and she stood silently beside what was once the royal bed, not wanting to move, and with ashes drifting down on to her from somewhere high above her. They left grey marks on her skin when she tried to rub them away, like small bruises. She imagined Aeneas' black ships sailing out of the harbour, even as the apricot and mauve of the new day broke over Carthage. I won't think of that, Elissa told herself. There's the child I'm carrying. Better to fix my mind on my baby. If a girl is born to me, I shall name her for the queen.

The poet has to speak and tell the tale
(even while sorrow guides his trembling hand)
of how the queen, bereft and stunned by grief,
climbed on the bed which she had set ablaze,
thinking to make of it her funeral pyre.
How then she grasped the Trojan's silver sword
and sheathed its blade for ever in her flesh.

How will we mourn the passing of our queen?
With tears and lamentations and sad songs.
For she was more than lovely, more than brave.
She was a queen whose strength and dignity
made Carthage known and glorious in the world.
Her sister weeps, and those who loved her once
mourn her grim fate as they remember her.

(from the poems of Iopas, singer at the court of Dido, Queen of Carthage).

Acknowledgements

Anne and Alastar Jackson have a wealth of knowledge they've been happy to share with me and I am grateful to them both.

Thanks also to Catherine Dolman, who knows everything there is to know about Dido; to Linda Sargent, Sally Prue, Laura Cecil, and to my family and friends for their support.